Thank you

for not Smoking

Arlo Flinn

Published by
Barfly Publications
Askerswell, Dorchester

Contact: arloflinn@thankyoufornotsmoking.co.uk
or visit: thankyoufornotsmoking.co.uk

ISBN 978-0-9561872-0-8

Cover by Joe Nava
at: joenava01@yahoo.co.uk

Printed and bound in Britain by Creeds, Broadoak,
Bridport, Dorset DT6 5NL
www.creedsuk.com

FOR CLARE

Thank you

"Selfishness is not living as one wishes to live, it is asking others to live as one wishes to live."

Oscar Wilde

 **1**

Something was wrong.

I was playing a selection of Neil Diamond hits on a white baby grand ... blinding white, bastard white, even the black keys, like an assault, stabbing at my eyes ... but I knew I had to keep playing. I had my Raybans pushed back on my head, the ones I found at Oxford Circus but I couldn't get to them to put them on because if I stopped the piano was going to explode. Someone had put a bomb in my piano ... and then Ian Paisley turned up. He wanted to bring his marching band through. They were waiting just over there, around the corner of some wrecked building. I tried to look where he was pointing but my eyes would only blink, blink, blink, like frames on a roll of film. He started shouting that it was his show, his turn now. I was trying to tell him I couldn't stop playing, I had to finish 'Sweet Caroline' or I wouldn't get paid and even without that there was the bomb ... and all the time this banging going on somewhere. I wanted him to find out what it was. It could be someone making another exploding piano ... and then a grappling hook caught the back of my collar and yanked me up into the air, out of danger and out of my dream and as I surfaced I was yelling for someone, anyone, to post my cheque on to me ...

But the banging was on the front door.

That was what was wrong. No-one came round on a Saturday morning. And someone was shouting up from the street. It sounded bad, whatever it was. I gave Electra a shove. She went to see what was up while I lay back and thought about where I'd learnt the Neil Diamond songs. I could still see my dream hands on the keyboard, knocking out the tunes. If I could do it in my sleep maybe I could get a job in a cocktail bar in Vegas and play to grateful American dowagers in spangly dresses instead of pissed tarmacking gangs in the Elephant and Castle. Electra came back and jumped in next to me.

"It's Miles," she said.

"Miles?"

"Miles Johnson. Your trombone friend."

"Where?"

"Coming up. He's hurt his leg."

I could hear him shuffling along the passage. He pushed the bedroom door open, leaning on the handle, and then he dragged his leg on in and stood at the end of the bed. He was wearing a coat over striped boxers.

"Your bell isn't working," he said.

"No. I pulled the wires out, to stop people coming round all the time."

"Oh. Sorry. I had to. Sally's thrown me out and you're just round the corner."

"Am I?"

I didn't know that. Come to think of it, I had no

idea where Miles lived. He always just turned up, sometimes with a van.

"Why's she thrown you out?" Electra asked him. I could see Miles didn't want to talk in front of her.

"D'you want to make us a cup of tea?" I said. She got back out of bed. Her bare feet made a happy little skippety sound on the stairs as she bounced down to the kitchen. We were still at the stage where she'd do anything I asked.

"Isn't she a bit ... young?" Miles said. "You know, to be ... staying?"

"It's a sleep-over," I said. "She's eighteen. She's cool."

"She's still at school."

"College. It's different. So why's Sally thrown you out? D'you want to sit?"

"Could I have a shower first, and borrow some clothes? I'm a bit pissy."

I shrugged. Fine. While he was in the bathroom I tried to remember Sally. She must've been to one of our gigs. Or one of the parties. I had a vague recollection of a lot of dark hair, and glasses? And old, much older than Miles, and she had a job, or a business or something. Miles came back with a towel round his waist. He sat on the edge of the bed and bent forwards to put his head in his hands, a pitiful demonstration of his deep despair ... but then he nearly tipped off onto the floor. The bed's quite high up and the mattress gives up under pressure so it's easy enough to do. I've done it myself.

"Sit in the chair," I said. "It's safer. So what's

up?"

"Sally's thrown me out."

"We've already covered that. Why's she thrown you out?"

This was getting boring already. Miles was alright but I hardly knew him. He was just a bloke I played with sometimes who came round sometimes and lived just round the corner, as it turned out, but that wasn't a good enough reason to wake me up on a Saturday morning when I should have been enjoying quality time with Electra. She'd gone to bed with her make-up on. She'd been too pissed to take it off. She'd been too pissed to do anything so I'd been looking forward to round about now because it always gave her a smutty, slutty look I found impossible to resist. Not that I needed to resist. I was getting as many in as was physically possible before the honeymoon phase was over. And then I had to pay attention and stop thinking about Electra. Miles was trying to tell me something.

" ... and he's in there till the end now," he was saying. I decided to let him run on. I'd catch up somehow. "Anyway, I know it happens. Of course I know. I've been to see him as much as possible. We all have, even Mum, and they've hardly spoken for years. But the thing is, I went to see him last night and he was so much worse, really gone downhill since Wednesday, and he made me promise to give up smoking. He could hardly talk. He can hardly breathe. His lungs are completely fucked but he went on and on about how I had to promise him I'd give up the fags and if only he'd stopped years ago and he knew what a risk he was taking but he just carried on anyway. Where's your girlfriend gone?"

"She'll be washing up."

"Oh." Miles shot me a look like I was a mean, nasty man, which was a bit much considering I'd taken him in and he was wearing one of my towels. And sitting on a chair in my bedroom.

"She likes doing it," I said. "She's playing Susie Homemaker. Don't worry, it won't last."

"Right. Anyway, he made me promise. It nearly finished him off but he wouldn't shut up till I'd sworn I'd stop. It was terrible. I was so fucked up after I left the hospital I went straight to the nearest pub and I got so pissed I ... I ... I ... "

The beat is crazy?

" ... I couldn't remember how to get home. And it was even worse because I wasn't smoking so I had nothing to straighten myself out with and maximum drinking time because I didn't have to stop to roll a fag. I had to get a cab in the end and Sally was screaming mad because she'd invited some friends round and I rolled up totally arseholed and embarrassed her and then I wet the bed. I had so much Stella I actually wet the bed and she went ape when she found out and when I tried to stop her throwing me out Kate attacked me with her hockey stick."

"Who's Kate?"

"Sally's daughter. She's eighteen."

Electra came in with a tray. She'd made tea and

toast.

"Kate who?" she said.

"Kate Kennedy," Miles said, thinking there was no way there would be a connection.

"She goes to my school," Electra said.

"College," I said.

Electra put the tray down on the bed and climbed back in beside me. She looked a mess, a gorgeous sexy mess with her eyes rubbed off and red still in the little dips on her lips and her knickers showing under one of my shirts. I wondered if there was any way I could get rid of Miles without seeming like a mean, nasty man ... probably not. Sadly.

"Would you come with me?" he said. " I've got to go back to see him this morning."

"Your father?" I said. It was a good guess.

"I can't face it on my own," he said. "Oh God, poor Dad, poor Dad, oh God oh God ... " etc.

He looked like he was about to fall apart so naturally I said yes. I couldn't have him wandering the public bars, looking for sympathy and a consolation shag. I needed him in one piece, on time, smart, sharp, up for it. Mr Bonwit from Ersatz Promotions was coming to see the gig tonight and it was way too late to start looking for a dep. And anyway, now I was thinking about it, Miles was the only trombone player I knew.

 **2**

Miles looked better in my clothes than he did in his own. Electra had dressed him for a Sunday afternoon tea party in Bulawayo, against all the evidence that we were in Clapham and it was still Saturday morning. It suited him. He had a kind of public school Prince Harry thing going I hadn't noticed before.

"You should wear that to the gig tonight," I told him. We were standing on the pavement outside my house. He was still crooked with his bruised leg.

"I can't play the trombone in a hat," he said.

"Have you ever tried?"

"Well, no."

"See? You need to lighten up," I said, and then I remembered we were off to visit his dying father. "After the funeral." That probably made it worse. "Sometime," I concluded, which left it more open.

Miles didn't seem too upset by this anyway. He was concentrating on his shoes, my shoes.

"I can't believe she'd throw me out," he said.

"That's women for you. You should try going out with a few teenagers. They're easier."

I meant to get along with, but it sounded like I thought they were all slags. Electra chose this very moment to leave the house. She must've heard me but she kissed me anyway and headed off all skippety like she did, a miniature hey-Tom Bombadil in purple ballet pumps. You could tell just from the way she walked she was away with the fairies.

"See what I mean?" I said. "So ... which hospital's your father in?"

"The Portesham."

I'd never heard of it. "How do we get there?"

"It's in Chelsea."

"Good. We can go for a drink after. Private then, is it?"

"Yeah."

We were walking towards the tube station. Miles was looking totally gutted. Maybe he just had the mother of all hangovers ...

"So is your family loaded?" I asked him, to try to snap him out of it. Money always does it for me. He could be in for a good whack in the near future.

"My dad's a doctor. He's got good insurance. God, I could do with a fag."

"Have one then."

"I can't."

"Buy some Polos. Your father won't be able to tell. He's ... er ... got other things on his mind."

"That's not the point. I promised him."

But I thought it was the point. We all say stuff under pressure we don't mean. What choice had Dr Johnson left his son? Maybe his only son? He had to agree to quit the fags, even if only for form's sake.

"Have you got any brothers or sisters?" I said.

"Yeah. Two of each."

"So what's all the fuss about? He's not going to know anyway, is he?" There were plenty of Johnson juniors to fill any gap that might or might not be left by a dead Miles. "My father smoked until he was fifty," I said.

"Then what happened?"

"He gave up." That was a lie, but a necessary one. He'd died in a car crash, fatally distracted by a malfunctioning cigar lighter. "I'm just saying you've got a margin of error before you get lung cancer yourself," I said cheerily. "How old are you?"

"Thirty one."

"See? Twenty years, Miles. You're alright for a while. Giving up smoking when you're really stressed doesn't work. You have to prepare yourself, get psyched up."

"How would you know?"

I was stamping out my cigarette in front of the tube station.

"I nearly gave up once. I realised I wasn't ready. It's better not to try than to try and fail. You don't want to set up a pattern." Miles stuck his hands deeper into his pockets, my pockets, to resist the packet of fags I was offering him. "Watch the side of the seams on those," I said. "They're genuine vintage."

The Portesham was in a chic Georgian square. If there were any crap add-on Nissen hut type buildings I couldn't see any, so it didn't look like a hospital.

It looked like someone's house, apart from all the nurses. I don't get the nurse thing. The uniform is bad and the shoes are worse. There was oppressive deep blue carpet everywhere, which seemed like a bad choice in a place where people go to leak a lot, and a matching ceiling with those discreet little recessed lights set in. It was like being in two sides of a plush coffin: you could almost hear the lid being screwed down ... almost, but that would be too much noise. It was the most silent place I'd ever been. I wanted to start shouting obscenities the minute we arrived.

Dr Johnson's room had more of the oppressive carpet. I stood by the door, trying to work it out, while Miles stood by the bed and waited for his father to realise he was there. We'd been standing around for a while when a nurse came in: Colleen, her name badge said. She fiddled around with various machines and left. Then she came back to ask us if we wanted tea or coffee. We stood around more. The silence was oppressive now, as well as the carpet. I wondered if you pulled it up and wrung it out, would you get a pile of all the sick noise, the bad arse noise, the screaming and wailing and the stink of the dying it had soaked up, the rot and the ...

Luckily at this point Colleen brought a tray in. We were still standing around when she came back again to clear it away.

"Your mother's been this morning," she told Miles.

"Right."

"She's just popped off to pick up a few things."
Popped off ... bad choice of words. Under the circumstances.

"Right," Miles said again.

"Your sister rang."

"Which one?"

"Helen, is it? She's coming in later, with your brother."

"Which one?"

I really couldn't see why any of this mattered. Dr Johnson was fully occupied soaking up the morphine from his drip while the carpet soaked up all the end-game groaning and ... and I had to stop with the carpet stuff. Enough carpet stuff. But it did seem a terrible shame he was missing out on the family reunion.

"Michael, is it?" Colleen was saying.

"And what did the doctor say?" Miles said. Colleen glanced at me, like maybe I should be asked to leave. "It's alright. He's an old friend," he told her

No, I'm really not. This was weird now. I was beginning to seriously regret coming.

"It's just a matter of time," she said. "I'm sorry."

Had anyone expected Dr Johnson to get better? I thought that was the point of terminal cancer: you died at the end. Miles was nodding though, so perhaps he, they, the Johnsons, had been secretly hoping for a miracle.

"How much time?" I said, before I had the sense to

realise this would include me in the family tragedy. Now Colleen was smiling at me. Miles was smiling at me. Shit. It was too late to back out. I was one of them, an honorary Johnson.

"It's hard to say. Not long," she said.

"Today, then?" I pressed her. I looked over at the patient, willing him to hang on a bit longer.

"It's hard to say," she said again. Had she detected my anxiety over the timing of this thing? Whatever, she picked up the tray and left.

We went on standing there.

"Perhaps you could shake him a bit," I said. "To let him know you're here." Because this was taking much longer than I'd expected. I had people to see, stuff to do ... but I also had to keep track of Miles. "He'd want to know you're here."

Miles thought about this for a while and then gave his father a prod on the shoulder. Nothing. Was he already dead? I watched his chest, to see if it was still moving. Hard to tell. Miles prodded him again. Still nothing.

"We could go for a drink and come back later," I said, although it would totally fuck up the day. "Let me try." I moved over nearer the bed. "Dr Johnson? Excuse me ... Dr Johnson?" It might have been the unfamiliar voice. He might have been planning on waking up anyway but he opened his eyes at this point, looked up at Miles and said, "Who are you?" From under his oxygen mask he sounded like he was talking through a loaf of bread.

"It's me, Dad," Miles said. "Miles."

"Ah," Dr Johnson said. "Who?"

"Miles. Your son."

"Ah. I can't see too well."

"No."

This was painful. Dr Johnson started to wheeze in a very alarming way, I suppose with the effort of talking like Miles had said. He gripped the blankets with his scrawny chicken-feet hands so you could see the bones through his skin: holding on for dear life. Literally.

"I haven't got long," he said. Now he sounded like a blocked vacuum cleaner.

"No," Miles said.

"But there's something I must tell you before I go. Miles, you have to stop smoking."

"You already told me, Dad. And I have, I promise."

But Dr Johnson wasn't convinced and he went into this whole speech about how stupid it was to smoke and how we all think we'll get away with it and yes, we all have to die but this was possibly the worst way to go etc. etc. He could only squeeze out two or three words at a time, in between long breaks for wheezing and gasping. I found I was holding my breath while he struggled for air so by the end of it I needed oxygen myself.

Miles tried to stop him in places, telling him that they'd been through this yesterday and that he'd already stopped smoking and his dad should save his breath. And every time he tried to stop him Dr Johnson would have to stop himself to say, "And what would I be saving my breath for?" Which took four or more goes to complete.

I personally thought Miles should stop interrupting. He was making it even harder for his father to get through his speech. But he did, thank Christ, and then he lolled back in a haze of morphine. I still felt dizzy and wondered if it was possible to get a contact high. Then a doctor came in and we had to stand in the corridor while he did something to poor old Dad. Miles wanted to stay on a bit longer but luckily Colleen said that too many people hanging around would wear his father down even faster so we were free to go. That wasn't how she phrased it, but it was what she meant.

"I need a drink," Miles said as soon as we'd escaped the deep blue half-coffin.

"Yeah. Are you alright?"

"No."

"That's what I thought. Come on. I know a great new bar down by the King's Road. They do lunchtime stand-up on a Saturday."

"I don't want to go to a comedy show," Miles said but I grabbed him by the arm and pulled him along the pavement in a matey, encouraging kind of way. He was too hung-over and depressed to seriously fight me off. He did try, but it was pathetic really.

"You've got to think about what your father would want for you," I told him, "out of respect for the old man. He'd want you to be out having a few beers, living the life."

I knew Miles hated me at that particular moment.

He needed someone to hate. But I also knew a couple of pints would see him over it.

"Trust me," I said, tightening my grip on his arm. "I know how to deal with this."

3

Imagine my surprise then when we got to the pub and I realised the medicine wasn't working. I was shocked. This had never happened before. After the first pint, instead of furring up around the edges, Dr Johnson's speech started to replay in my head. I could hear his voice. After the second I couldn't shut him up. His poor old lungs were struggling for air ... gasp, wheeze, suck, gasp ...

If I was feeling bad, Miles had to be far worse. We were leaning on the bar, watching the smoke from my cigarette drift up towards the nicotine ceiling. There is a paint called Nicotine ... check it out if you don't believe me ... but this wasn't it. This was a once lively red, now turned liver brown by a nicotine glaze ... like the inside of Dr Johnson's lungs.

I had to pull myself together. I was no use to Miles like this.

"How about a whiskey?" I said. "Chase the blues away."

"No thanks," Miles said. "Could you hold your fag away? It's making me salivate."

"Sorry." I put it out. "It's more the hospital than your father," I said. "It's a very depressing place."

"Is it?"

"Yeah. No offence, but all that money makes me want to join a revolution."

"What?"

"It's obscene. No offence, but it is."

"What?"

"When you think of children dying in Africa," I said, which I never did until I wanted to make a socio-political point. Or piss people off.

"But you're really rich," Miles said. He seemed to be coming out of his slump.

"No I'm not."

"Yes you are. You live in a fuck off huge house in the most expensive street in Clapham and you have more parties than anyone I know. You get caterers in, for fuck's sake. You serve champagne. Well, you don't. You get some goon in a tux to do it for you. Don't fucking tell me you're poor."

He was well and truly out of his slump now.

"It's not my house," I said.

"Whose house is it, then? Barman, two more pints and two whiskeys here, please."

"It's my sister's. Maybe you should slow down."

"Well how come she's got so much money? Where is she? I've never met her."

"You can meet her this afternoon if you want."

"How come she's so fucking loaded, then?"

Miles was more cheerful now he was actively angry. He had a happy little flush running from the neck up and he was waving his pint around to emphasise his point.

"We inherited when my father died. Watch your

pint there."

"You told me your father was still alive you fucking bastard bollocks."

"No I didn't. I told you he gave up smoking. He died in a car crash."

"So what happened to your share of the loot?"

I shrugged. It said it all really, because Miles was suddenly satisfied by my explanation. Or too pissed already to care.

"My sister used hers to buy the house," I said. "She was always more sensible than me. She had a job anyway, so she had to stay in London."

"Where is she now?"

"Richmond." I could tell Miles was thinking property empire. I could tell he was thinking you jammy bastard because it did look like I was the luckiest piano player in town. "She's in rehab," I said. "She lost it when her boyfriend left her. That was after she made her third million. It didn't improve her personality. He was a nice bloke but all that money turned her into a total shit. She might've always been that way ... you know, hidden underneath ... but once she got the account at Coutts there was no stopping her."

"Oh," Miles said. "Are you going to have another fag?"

"Yeah."

"Blow it this way, will you? I'm beginning to see your point."

"About what?"

"About giving up. It won't stop me dying. Like

your father."

"No. But stick it out for a while. You never know, you might actually do it."

I was beginning to sense something of a role reversal. I was being sensible. Miles was being drunk and irresponsible. I leant back against the bar and looked around the room. Miles was on his fourth pint. It didn't matter. Better shit-faced now than later. There were hours of sobering up time to go before the gig. I wondered if anyone in the pub had noticed the steady type at the bar with his dead-beat drunken friend ... his well-dressed dead-beat drunken friend.

Then I noticed that there wasn't anyone much to notice: the place was almost empty. Miles had turned around too.

"It's not very popular, your comedy lunch," he slurred.

"It'll fill up later," I said. I tried to remember the last time I'd been. I was sure the place had been packed. Yeah, because it had taken an indecent amount of time to get served. And you could hardly see the comedians for heads in the way.

"Where's the stage?" Miles said.

This was a good point. There wasn't a stage.

"Maybe they've got those headset mic things," I said. "So they can work the room."

"Ha ha ha," Miles laughed ironically. His pint slopped on the bar. The barman was looking over.

"Let's get a table," I said. I steered him to a table in a corner. The barman was watching us.

"You need to sit still for a while," I told him.

"Why? I'm fine." He tried to turn round in his chair to yell across the pub for two more whiskeys but somehow he lost his balance and the chair fell over with him on it. "My fucking father's dying," he shouted up from the floor.

This was clearly not a good enough explanation to satisfy the barman. He was coming out from behind the bar, coming over to ask us to leave, when the music started ... Lady Marmalade ... and the strippers filed out of the back somewhere. I could see him hesitate. Maybe he thought the strippers would distract Miles. Maybe he didn't want to spoil the show. Whatever, he retreated and stood scowling in front of his tacky optics.

One of the strippers saw Miles on the floor and made straight for him. Poor cow. She must've thought he was going to be an easy touch. She wriggled around in front of him for a while, all fake tan and bad hair, swinging the fringes on her white cheerleader bikini, and then she stepped over him, legs spread, so you could see her shaving rash. Miles just lay there, protesting that he wasn't drunk and kind of squinting up at her, like it hurt him to look. It probably did. The view must have been as bad as it could be from the floor. And then she took off her top half, one strap, two straps, wait for it boys, like we were really interested in what she had to show us ... voulez-vous coucher avec moi? No thanks, love ... leaning forward line by line, singing along, dangling her tits above his face. I could tell he

24

wasn't in the mood. He was asking her to go away but she got in closer and closer and then he yelled:

"My God, that's the worst breast enhancement I've ever seen."

Which was how he would say it, being a doctor's son. The stripper took it badly although he was right: it was a terrible job. She needed to sue her surgeon. Unfortunately this had also occurred to Miles, who was yelling:

"Fucking Jesus Christ, I hope you didn't pay for that. You should see a lawyer."

Now the stripper was yelling too ... you bastard, fuck off, I hate you etc ... but she did back off and then she started to cry and as she wiped her nose on the back of her hand I could see she'd done a line or two before the show. The barman was on his way over and then some psycho gorilla appeared from nowhere and dragged Miles to his feet, probably to hit him, but as soon as he let him go he fell over again. I checked the time: 12:47, for God's sake.

"Look," I said to the gorilla. "His father's dying and he's given up smoking. He doesn't normally get this drunk. Cut him some slack this once, would you?"

Which might've worked, only Miles had spotted something else he was unhappy with.

"And you've got cellulite," he roared at the sobbing stripper. "Plastic tits and fucking cellulite. Why don't you get a job where you keep your clothes on?"

I'd never seen this side of Miles before. Come to

think of it, I'd never seen him drunk before. Psycho gorilla was dragging him by the collar ... my collar ... towards the door while he shouted that he wanted to see the comedy, his father was dying and it wasn't funny. I suppose he was still drunk from last night, which was how come he'd got so out of hand so quickly, and without the nicotine to keep things under wraps ...

Now we were on the pavement. Psycho gorilla was looking for any excuse to punch either of us but I was too far away and Miles was still on the floor. In the end it was the barman who had the real nasty streak. He poured what was left of Miles' pint over his face, standing on his arm while he tried to twist out of the way. Then they lost interest and went back inside.

I sat down on the kerb next to Miles and lit a fag.

"Jesus, Miles," I said. "You need to calm down."

"Give me a fag," he said. "I'll start again tomorrow."

Did I really care? Of course not, but it could be that the not-smoking thing was all that was keeping him together. Or together as he was, which was not very at all. And anyway, I was discovering a real pleasure in restraint. I wanted to see what would happen next, in a kind of lab rat way: Miles under the microscope. It was just a shame there was no-one around to have a bet with.

"No," I said. "You've come this far. Think of your father. By tonight you'll have done twenty-four hours. Let's get some coffee and go and see

Jessica."

"Who's Jessica?"

"My sister."

"No-one in rehab's called Jessica."

There was nothing to say to this so I sat there and finished my fag, carefully blowing the smoke away from him, while happy shoppers walked by with bags from Gap and Next: normal people.

"Hey, alright mate?" someone said. It was Tim, a drummer friend. "You coming to the comedy?"

"We've just been," I said. "It didn't go too well."

Tim looked at the pub behind us. Then he looked at me. There was no-one in behind his shiny blue eyes.

"In there?" he said. "It's not in there. It's at the Gun and Garters. You alright there, Miles?"

And he went off down the street without waiting for an answer, doing his beat box impersonation. Except a beat box isn't a person. But it might be more of a person than Tim.

"What's his problem?" Miles said.

"I'll tell you what," I said. "You may be really fucked up but at least you're not shovelling coke up your nose all bloody day long. Come on, you're going to have to get up. We'll never get a cab like this."

 **4**

I bought a litre of Evian and poured it over Miles'
head. He looked better. It sobered him up by a
couple of pints as well. Now he was sitting stiffly in
the back of a cab, eyes front, clearly shaken by the
way his Saturday morning had panned out.

"I am so sorry," he said again. "I just don't know
what happened. I never do anything like that. Ever.
I've never been thrown out of a pub in my life. Do
you think I should go back and apologise?"

"No," I said.

"I'll drop them a card sometime then, just to say
how sorry I am."

"Don't bother. They don't care. They like a bit of
action."

"I'm so sorry. You must be so embarrassed."

I was glad he'd reverted to type, the nicely brought
up doctor's son of solid middle class values. It was
how our relationship worked. I felt we were over
the worst.

"Forget it," I said. "We all lose the plot
sometimes."

"But I am so sorry."

"Pull over here, would you?" I said to the cabbie.
"I've just got to do something," I told Miles. "Don't
move, alright?"

Angus was jumpy, much more jumpy than his usual gibbering self.

"Who's that in the taxi?" he said as soon as he opened the door. He didn't wait for an answer. He sprinted back across the hall and into his sitting room, back to his position by the tall double windows, floor to ceiling behind acres of lace curtains. They'd come out of a chateau somewhere, Angus had once told me. Sometimes I wondered if he was gay. He twitched one aside now and scanned the street through his binoculars.

"It's no-one," I said.

"What's his name then, this no-one? I told you, don't bring anyone round."

"I haven't brought him round. He doesn't know where I am."

Visits to Angus were always hard work but I was obliged to keep piling on the charm. There was too much riding on him to let him know he was the most paranoid twat I'd ever met.

"Are you expecting someone?" I asked him, a stupid question but I had to say something. The arrangement we had going was straightforward business but for some reason I always had to dress it up as something else. So did he. I didn't want to talk to Angus. I was sure he didn't want to talk to me but we had to have our pre-deal chat. I was watching his back, flipping through my Angus file for something else to say when it occurred to me why we had to do this, to dress it up: naked, the whole thing stank.

"Did you get to Tangier then?" I said. The last

time I'd seen him he'd told me he had to go to visit his mother in Tangier. She was ill.

"No," he said. "There were no fucking flights. I might go next week."

"No flights?" I said.

"No. No good flights. These fucking airlines. They think you've got time to travel, via Madrid, via fucking Malaga, get a mother-fucking ferry ... I can't do it, man. In and out, that's me."

I wondered what his girlfriends made of this attitude. Or his boyfriends. I walked across the room to examine a gilt mirror hanging above the mantelpiece, to distract myself from the invading image.

"Is this new?" I said. Angus liked his antiques. His flat was stuffed with them.

"Yeah. I just got it restored."

"Where's it from?" I meant was it French or Italian or what.

"E-Bay," he said. "I buy on-line now. I don't have time to go shopping."

He sounded angry, like I'd accused him of something.

"No," I said. He didn't have time to go shopping. It was taking all his time to watch the street outside.

"Are you expecting someone?" I asked him. Again, except this time I actually wanted to know.

"Why? Did you hear something?" he said.

He twisted round to look at me but he still had his binoculars glued to his face. I fought off the instinct to dive behind his Chesterfield. It was like having a gun pointed at me, which has only ever happened by mistake but even then it's rarely a good place to find yourself. Or a comfortable one. I decided it was time to do the deal and leave, before whoever it was he was expecting turned up.

"No," I said. "I didn't hear anything. So ... I've got to get going." He felt in his trouser pocket and handed me Jessica's order. "See you in two weeks then? The band's got a gig tonight at Louis' Place if you're out. The jazz club?"

"Ah, Louis," Angus said, like he knew him. It had never crossed my mind that there was a Louis. I'd always thought it was just a cheap shot at credibility, mainly because the club was run by someone called Mike. But Angus wouldn't have time to see a band anyway.

"No-one's throwing up," he said.

I left him with his binoculars and his expensive antique furniture and his gay-boy curtains and went to see what Miles was up to.

The cabbie had driven off. I couldn't blame him. Miles was white and shaking. I sat him on a bench in the bijou garden outside Angus's building and waited for him to pull himself together.

"It was the whiskey," he said. "I'm alright now."

"That's good," I said, "because this isn't the best place to be sitting. Can you walk?"

"Yeah, if I had something to eat."

"We should leave. Come on." I pulled him up onto his feet and linked his arm through mine. I was glad to see his vomit had missed my shoes. "There's a sandwich shop down the road. I'll get you some lunch and you'll be fine."

I looked back before we turned the corner. Angus was watching us from his window. I could see the sun flashing across his binoculars, the poor sad fuck.

I flagged down another cab and we were heading for Richmond. Now Miles was fed he was asking questions, just wanting to make normal noise. He didn't really want any answers.

"Where did you go?" he said. "I had to pay the cab. He wouldn't wait."

"I'll pay you back. I had to see someone."

"Who?"

"A friend of Jessica's."

"She lives back there?"

Miles was impressed. It was an impressive building.

"It's flats," I said.

"All the same ... "

"And you didn't see me go in there, alright?"

"Fine. Why? Is she famous or something?"

"No."

"Is she coming to the gig tonight?"

"Jessica? No. She doesn't go out."

"I meant her friend."

"It's a he. And he isn't coming to the gig. He doesn't go out much either."

"Oh. Michael's coming, my brother. He got

divorced last year."

"Michael would not want to meet any of Jessica's friends, no matter how desperate he is," I said. "They all work in the City."

"So does he."

"He probably knows them already then. He definitely wouldn't want to meet Angus."

"Who you just went to see? Angus who?"

"McNab," I said, thinking there was no way there would be a connection.

"Does he work in the City?"

"He used to. He's branched out. He deals in futures." It was the first thing that came into my head. I tried not to laugh but Miles knew something was up.

"Futures?" he said.

Jesus. He was relentless, the Colombo of the casual conversation.

"Sort of. He's Jessica's dealer." It was easier to tell him than to invent a pile of crap that I'd then have to work at remembering. He was wearing me out. "But don't let her know you know," I said. "It's her little secret."

"But why did you go to see her dealer? She's in rehab."

Suddenly not Colombo. He wasn't getting it at all.

"It helps her keep a lid on it," I said.

"But you're not taking her anything? Are you? You are taking her something?"

"It's what she wants."

Miles was shocked. Shocked and appalled but at least he'd shut up.

"Look," I said after a while. "She's doing what she can. If she leaves rehab she'll be destitute within a year. Or dead. This way she can hang on to her assets and ... you know ... slowly sort herself out. It's a gradual thing with her. She tried cold turkey. It didn't go too well."

"So you live in her house while she lives in a clinic?"

"Not really a clinic. She asked me to. Think of me as her caretaker and you'll be about right."

I wasn't going to tell Miles that Jessica kept me on a salary, that I got a bonus for running her supplies out to Richmond, that her brilliantly invested millions kept the house up, me up, her up and her hippy rehab place happy. Which sounded fine, except I knew it wasn't. And so did Angus. And now Miles knew what a crock of shit it was too.

"Anyway, I got you something," I said, to lighten the atmosphere. A taxi is the wrong place for intense introspective gloom. I pulled Jessica's order out of my pocket and broke off a scratchy lump of skunk. "For later. You promised your dad you'd give up the fags, right? I bet he didn't mention the grass."

"But that's stealing from your own sister," Miles said.

"For her own good," I said. He frowned. This was a tricky one. "It's best not to go into the ethics," I advised him. "Believe me, I've tried. It's a minefield. Here we are, anyway. Can I borrow my hat?"

 5

I realised my mistake as soon as we sat down in the conservatory. This was not a good place for Miles: everyone was smoking, or almost everyone. All the residents had a fag between their nasty yellow fingers. Most of the visitors were smoking too, stressed to the edge of junkydom themselves by the sorry state of their inmate. I refrained from lighting up, for Miles' sake, and reflected that it was still better for him to be with me than wandering the public bars of Clapham in his pissy boxers.

"Can't we sit somewhere else?" he said.

"This is where the visitors go," I said. "We're not allowed in the rest of the house."

Miles was counting.

"How many people stay here?" he said.

"Don't know. Twenty?"

"Then they're all in here. The rest of the house must be empty."

"The rest of the house always is empty," I said. "This is the smoking area."

"Why can't we sit in it? If it's empty?"

The rest of the house, a vast Victorian pile, was reserved for the privacy of the residents. They had to have their privacy. It was essential to their recovery. I told Miles this.

"But they're not getting any privacy if they're all in here," he said. "It's so smoky."

"Yes. That's because it's the smoking area," I said. "They've got to have one vice left to them, Miles. Everyone needs one good vice."

"Yes," he said, biting into his thumb nail. "What d'you make of Colleen?"

"Your father's nurse? She's alright."

"I was going to ask her to the gig tonight. For Michael."

He seemed deeply concerned by his brother's lack of bird. This was probably displacement activity, something that Electra was always telling me I did. But never mind about that now.

"My father had a bay mare called Colleen," I said. "She was the biggest bitch."

She also kicked my mother and broke her back but it seemed unlikely that Colleen the nurse would do this to Michael so there was no point in mentioning it. Miles had enough on his plate already.

"You're making that up," he said.

"I'm not. We always had horses, the bastard things. We only sold them to make room for more. We had to go to the races and watch them run. And that was after the hunting all day and mucking out the bloody stables and cleaning out the troughs and walking the sodding hound puppies and on and on with it." I realised I'd gone very Irish. I took a deep breath. "The only decent thing was the piano in the back hall." Now I sounded like a pathetic neglected child. Which I was, in a way. An Irish way. "It was

36

always fucking freezing," I concluded. "Even in the summer."

"So shall I ask her or not?"

"If you want. Here's Jessica."

Jessica was weaving her way towards us through the groups of cane chairs and coffee tables.

"Wow," Miles said.

"Really not," I warned him. She looked better than she had in a long time, I had to admit, if you liked spiteful cadavers.

"She looks like Nicole Kidman," Miles said.

"She doesn't. She looks like a corpse. She hasn't eaten anything since she was three."

"Hi," Jessica said, sitting down and tucking her legs up underneath her. This accentuated her starving pixiness to maximum effect. She pulled her sleeves down over her bony fingers and shivered.

"I'm Jessica," she said to Miles. "You came all this way to see me."

Except he could live in Richmond, I thought, so he might have travelled an exhausting full half mile to get here.

"This is Miles," I said. "He's in the band."

"Oh," Jessica said. Interesting. A musician. A twitching musician who was eating his thumb. She was locking on with terrifying accuracy. I could see it happening. Maybe I should've left him at home ... but I had to keep him together. It was all about the gig. The enormity of my error took a grip ... how could I have been so stupid? Miles and Jessica ...

Jessica and Miles ... Jessica Johnson. The names went together perfectly, a fact that would occur to her in no time at all ...

"What's up?" she asked him, American style. "Are you staying at the house?"

"I might have to," Miles said, "if that's alright with you."

"Sure," she said, more as a breathy sigh than a word. "My big brother's in charge."

Shit. I tuned out. I've never enjoyed horror as a genre. In his depleted state Miles was easy meat to someone as comprehensively fucked up as Jessica. This was going to be a massacre. Sally had been a fool to throw him out. What was a bladder-full of Stella leaked into her mattress compared to the bleached skeleton she'd get back now when they made it up? It could take him years to recover. And then it occurred to me that maybe Sally wouldn't take him back. Maybe she had no plans to make it up with Miles. She might be glad to see him gone. She might have been waiting for an opportunity to dump him. On me. Shit.

"So how's your programme going?" I said to Jessica.

"Fine," she said, without breaking her eyes away from Miles.

She liked a bit of posh. But not too posh. She liked Miles then.

Why hadn't I seen this one coming? He'd never go back to Sally now, even if she'd have him. I'd seen her do this to blokes before. It was a helpless thing,

38

a spindly, frail, look-after-me junky-fairy thing. It knocked them flat, if that was what they went for. Which Miles clearly did. He'd realise in the end that she was actually the velociraptor daughter of the Prince of Darkness and not the sister of his dearest friend at all. But this would only be after she'd eaten the living flesh from his writhing bones and sucked out the marrow while he screamed in agony for Sally, Sally, Sally ...

"We're going for a walk," Jessica said, poking me with her pointy boot and shattering my Gothic fantasy. "Miles can't handle the smoke in here. Are you coming?"

So soon? This was how I handed over her order, as we strolled through the shrubbery. I followed them out through the conservatory doors.

" ... amazing. I love these coincidences," she was saying now.

"Yah, yah," Miles said. He never said yah.

I trailed along behind them. Jessica rolled a cigarette, now that we were outside and it wouldn't trouble Miles, getting him to hold the tobacco, hold the lighter, hold the Rizlas. She blew the smoke away from him and swept her hair back with her free hand and gave him a look, That Look, that look which said I know you'll forgive my weakness because you're so, so much, so very much stronger than me.

I know men are stupid.

I know I'm stupid but I still can't believe anyone would fall for this.

Women hated her. They saw through her. They didn't trust her. Quite right, too. Neither did I.

We wandered across the lawn and into the shrubbery. Jessica steered Miles to our usual place and then she turned to me, light and bouncy in her fairy-cowboy boots. I removed my hat to reveal her order ... but I was unprepared. I had no idea she was going to pull this one so soon.

"I don't want it," she said. "I'm really sorry. I just know that now is the right time. I'm going to get better."

She wouldn't have expected a reaction from me. She knew I wouldn't believe a word of it, not for a nanosecond. But then she wasn't saying it to me. She was saying it to Miles. The trap clanged shut. I heard it ... or was that a 747 crashing into Bromley? Hard to tell the difference. She flashed me a look. She knew I knew full well what she was doing.

"Right," I said.

Miles was standing at a discreet distance, misty-eyed, done for. Jessica did a half-twirl ... even lighter now in her bloody boots ... shrugged a naughty fairy shrug to apologise for all the trouble she'd caused and exited left, blowing a kiss to Miles as she went.

"Wow," he said.

"Not wow," I said.

"Aren't you pleased for her? That she doesn't want the stuff?"

The stuff? The stuff? I felt the will to live draining

away.

There was no point in trying to explain to Miles what she was up to. There was no point because he would never believe that wispy junky-fairy could be so cruel as to suck him in (and off. I had been reliably informed that Jessica gave great head, but only once per victim, which was another of her poisonous little tricks) ... that she could be so callous as to let him think that he was the one man in the world who could make her straight, right, sane, pregnant, only to find her diving, after a brief spell of honeymoon, straight back into her bad old habits. He would go with her for her abortion, hold her hand, blame himself for her coke-mountain, Wild Turkey, forty-a-day consumption and then in no time at all she'd be back in rehab. When I got to this point I cheered up. There was always something to look forward to.

"I'm thrilled," I said. "Now we've got to run the gauntlet all the way back to Clapham with a nice little stash of class A."

"Why don't you just chuck it?" he said.

"Have you lost your mind? Come on. I'll ring for a cab from the end of the drive."

We walked along together. I had been press-ganged into his family this morning. Now he had joined mine, but willingly. He felt closer to me, I could tell. I moved to the right-hand side of the drive. He followed. He was so smitten I was the next best thing to Jessica.

"Why don't you like her?" he said, a concerned

almost-brother trying to mend a family feud.

"I adore her. She's divine," I said. He smiled happily. He felt the same way. "It's just a brother sister thing. That's how we are."

"I'm coming to see her tomorrow," he said.

"Really?" We'd see about that.

"Yah. So ... how long's she been here?"

"On and off, I'd say three years. They're quite ... relaxed. There was Clouds before that. They're not relaxed. They expect you to take it seriously. It wasn't Jessica's style." Little clue dropped in there. Had he noticed? Had he fuck. "She's been cleaning up for a long time," I said. Do the maths, sucker.

"But now she's finally going to do it." Miles was ecstatic.

"Yeah. Amazing." You poor infant. I hoped it would be a quick destruction. It was less painful that way.

"Can I have a cigarette now?" he said.

"No. We'll have some grass later." But only if you're very, very good. My God, he was learning the tricks fast.

"I really will start again tomorrow. Giving up, I mean."

"Look, Miles," I said. "Rehab places always have this effect. You see a bunch of the permanently lunched and it makes you feel so sorted you think you don't have a thing to worry about. But that's like comparing ... Jack the Ripper with Genghis Khan." That was a terrible example. I kept going anyway. "It doesn't make him any less of a murderous bastard."

"Which one?" he said. He was sulky now.

"You know what I mean," I said. "Just don't smoke. Be strong for Jessica."

He was happy again. "You're right," he said.

We stood at the end of the drive, waiting for a cab.

"You do want her to get better?" Miles asked me.

"Yeah of course."

Of course not, you idiot. Everything works like this. Everyone's happy. Or as happy as they're going to be. The mood I was in, maybe I should chuck the order. Or at least the coke.

But then maybe not. Who really knows what's next?

6

"We need food next," I said. "Hot food."

We were on the pavement outside my house. The sky had turned gunmetal grey. There'd be a storm later.

"What about Angelina's?" Miles said.

We went there sometimes after gigs. They had a pretty relaxed attitude towards minor details like turn out. I checked Miles over. He looked alright, as long as you didn't get in close.

"We'll walk," I said. "The air will do you good."

"Can I get changed first?" he said.

"You're fine. We'll do that later. After a kip."

"But I have to go and see my dad again. It's almost five now."

"We'll go on from the restaurant. There's time. Then we can come back, shower, change. We don't have to set up till ten."

"That's a lot of taxis. I'll have to owe you." That suited me. He was jogging along, doing his best to keep up. "I didn't know you walked," he said.

"So how do I get from the bar to my piano?"

"I meant really walk. I ... "

What he really meant was he thought I was nothing but a lounge lizard. Which was a fair assessment, considering he only ever saw me in bars and

44

nightclubs.

"There's a lot you don't know about me," I said. I was joking but it sounded surprisingly sinister. Miles looked unsettled by this ... or maybe he was just out of breath.

"The hound puppies," he said. At least he was keeping up there. "Did Jessica walk the hound puppies too?"

"Oh yes. She was the all-Ireland Hound Walking Junior Champion in 1989."

"Really? Wow."

Jesus, what a twat. All the same, you couldn't help liking him.

Angelina's was busy. It was dark and cramped and it smelt great. We got a table at the back and ate breadsticks and talked about the gig. I asked Miles if he was up for a tour if it went well tonight. I was praying it would. I needed this to work out. I needed a break from Electra. I needed a change of scenery. I needed to stop being my sister's gofer but without any other work ... if you could call it that ... I was stuck. A tour would be perfect.

"I don't know," Miles said. "I've got to work things out with Sally. And I've got my job."

"What job?"

"I teach. At a prep school in Chiswick."

"They learn trombone at prep school? Aren't they a bit ... long?"

I imagined his little pupils struggling with their short little arms, red-faced, sweaty, close to tears while merciless Miles beat time on a metal music stand. There was no future in it.

"I don't teach trombone. I teach French and History."

Damn it. I broke a breadstick.

"What if it doesn't work out with Sally?"

"And there's Dad. D'you want some wine?"

I ordered some house red and considered Miles' availability. O.K. I needed Sally to dump him, permanently. I needed Dr Johnson to die quickly. And I needed the prep school in Chiswick to sack him. Or burn down. There was a good chance of the first two working out this weekend but I wasn't so sure about the third. The house red arrived. I dipped a breadstick in it.

"And there's Jessica," Miles said. "I know you shouldn't get straight into another relationship ..." He waited for me to say something, I sucked my breadstick. " ... but ... you know ... sometimes that's just how the timing goes."

"So you don't want to get back with Sally?"

"I think it was over anyway, even without the piss."

This was good. This was what I wanted. But not Jessica. I had to get him away from Jessica. She would fuck everything up. She always did.

"You should have a break before you get into anything new," I said. A tour-length break. "How long have you been with Sally?"

"Four years."

Our plates of Bolognese arrived.

"Definitely a break. A complete change while you get stuff out of your system. Otherwise you'll take all your crap with Sally into your relationship with Jessica. She couldn't handle it. She's not that strong."

"No." Miles was nodding his head while he sucked up his spaghetti.

"And if it's right with Jessica you don't need to rush in to anything."

Miles had stopped sucking up his spaghetti. He was staring over my shoulder.

"It's Sally," he said. The half-sucked spaghetti quivered like tentacles. Disgusting.

"Where?" I turned around. The restaurant was too full to see anything much and we were behind a fish tank anyway. Miles took a big slug of wine.

"The fucking bitch," he said.

"Where?" I said. "Could you finish your mouthful?"

"Sorry. There. Sitting down with some bloke. There."

I stood up and looked over the fish tank. The table caught on my belt and tilted towards Miles. He managed to catch the carafe of wine and his glass but his spaghetti slid off his plate into his lap.

"Sorry," I said. "D'you mean the dark girl in the red top?"

"Of course. You know who Sally is." He was putting his spaghetti back on his plate now.

"Yeah. Look, don't jump to conclusions. It could be a friend. How are my trousers?"

"Most of it went on the napkin. That's not a friend. Look at the way they're looking at each other. But don't stand up again." He took another big slug of wine.

I twisted round and watched them through the lobsters. They were holding hands across the table, but in a patting sort of way.

"He could be a friend," I said. "Or a colleague. Where does she work?"

"She's got her own catering business," Miles said snappily.

"Has she? She doesn't look like a cook."

"She's done the catering for two of your parties, for fuck's sake. That was how we met, you and me. I was helping her out once." I think he was quite offended that I couldn't immediately place her. "What do cooks look like anyway?"

"I don't know. Either fat or dead skinny." Sally was neither of these things. She was actually quite fit in a bare-faced, scrubbed kind of way. Odd that I didn't remember her. "I'm always wrecked at my own parties," I said. "That's probably why I didn't recognise her."

I was planning on having some more wine while I thought about how I'd missed such a good-looking girl ... but Miles had drunk it all.

"Shall I go and say hallo?" I said. "I could get the bloke's name."

"No. You could get some more wine."

"Come on, Miles. You've already been pissed once today."

"Give me a fag then."

"You can't smoke in here. We're about to go and see your father. You've got to keep it together."

"Waiter," Miles roared. "More wine here."

Which of course Sally heard. The whole restaurant heard. She looked over but she couldn't see us behind the fish tank. I was keen to avoid another incident.

"Look Miles," I said. "I'm sure there's an explanation. It's a bit of a coincidence that you're both in here. I'm sure she's gone out of her way to avoid you. He's probably a client. Or one of her suppliers. Does she do much with asparagus?" A vague memory of a tart was teasing my taste buds: pale pastry, very yellow eggs under the lamp on the sideboard. "He looks like an asparagus grower to me."

I said this to distract him although Sally's bloke could easily have been an asparagus grower. He was slightly hunched, like he spent a lot of time looking at the ground. Unfortunately Miles didn't want to be distracted. His ego was outraged.

"Out of her way?" he shouted. "Out of her fucking way? We live across the fucking street, for fuck's sake. Or she does. I don't live anywhere and my father's dying."

So why had he suggested Angelina's? He was checking up on her. He must have suspected he already had a replacement ... oh God. Now he was crying. He really was the most inept and instant drunk I'd ever met, and no fun at all. Sally was in no doubt now about who was shouting from behind the fish tank. I would've run if I were her but she didn't. She stood up and came over.

"Remember," I told Miles. "You said you didn't want to get back together. Think of Jessica"

Sally was standing by our table now. I think she was about to launch into a verbal assassination of poor old Miles when she noticed me. I raised my hat, which I'd forgotten to remove from my head.

"Good afternoon, Sally," I said. I didn't attempt to stand up, what with the spaghetti still on the table.

"I might have known," she said. She put out her hand and ... shit ... lifted Jessica's order from the top of my head. It was like being back at school. "Miles ... I just don't know where to start," she said. She threw the little silver package onto the table and flounced off.

"It's a piece of birthday cake," Miles shouted after her. "From a charity birthday party. That's what we've been doing all day. They've got Downes syndrome, you know."

Oh God. She was coming back.

"No, it's not," she said. "We all know what it is. What else would your depraved, decadent, drunken friend have under his hat?"

Nice alliteration. And spontaneous too. Unless she'd been waiting for a chance to say it ...

"It's birthday cake," Miles said. He'd turned into a sullen child. He snatched it up and stuffed it in his mouth before Sally could grab it.

"Do tell me, Sally," I said. "What does your friend

do for a living?"

"Oh fuck off," she said and left.

"You'd better spit that out," I told Miles.

He fished it out of his mouth. It was a soggy mess inside the foil wrapper.

"It's come undone," he said.

"We'd better get to the hospital fast," I said.

"Am I going to die?"

"Get a grip, Miles. I meant to see your father. Before the top of your head comes off."

7

I stuffed Miles into a cab. He was sweating. I had déjà vu.

"My heart's racing," he said.

I sat with my back to the driver and ignored his latest crisis, carefully unwrapping Jessica's order. There was the skunk, of course, a modest tangle of spiky buds. There was also a mulch of wraps of whatever. Two, maybe three of them, had started to unwrap. It was hard to say how much had leaked out.

"What is it?" Miles said.

"Don't know. Coke, but I know Jessica's been having trouble sleeping so there could be something else as well ... you know, uppers, downers." It sounded quaint. I was trying to sort out the mess but it was guesswork really.

"Like what?" Miles said. "What kind of downers?"

"I don't know. This is out of my territory. I'm just the delivery boy." I glanced up at Miles, to see how he took this. Shit. He looked more like he was going sideways. "Hopefully they'll cancel each other out," I said hopefully, easily. "There's nothing to worry about."

So what sends you sideways? MDF? No no no. It was MD something, I was sure, if I had to tell a doctor later. I was seriously regretting not having paid more attention to Jessica's drug habit.

"But why isn't it wrapped up properly?" Miles said.

"Angus always was sloppy. The thing is, Miles, you're not supposed to put it in your mouth. Or chew it."

"I was pretending it was birthday cake."

"I don't think Sally believed you."

"It was worth a try."

"Whatever. How are you feeling now?"

"Better. Good actually."

That'll be the coke then. With luck he only got a dab, just enough to sharpen him up. I folded the silver paper back around the mulch and put it back under my hat. We might be needing some adjustment later.

"Why does she have so many?" Miles said.

"Wraps? It's how she rations herself. It's alright. You only got a taste. Believe me, that's a tube of Smarties compared to ... "

I gave up. Miles wasn't listening. He was staring out of the cab window at the pretty streets, the intriguing shops, the elegant lamp posts ...

"I never realised before what a beautiful city London is," he said. "Look at it."

I reflected that while Angus was sloppy and also borderline insane, his gear was always primo quality. The downside of this was that he was responsible for more accidental overdoses than any other dealer in town. But there was nothing to be done now. At least Miles was happy.

The hospital visit was a bad bet. I'd known this before we left Angelina's. I still knew it as I steered Miles towards the swishy doors. It had crossed my mind to give it up and come back later as straight, clean, sober citizens but that might take some time and with Dr Johnson about to shuffle off it could be Miles' last chance.

Was I bastard enough to keep a son from his dying father?

I checked my conscience ... er ... no, can't find it.

But actually he did look alright. I briefed him on what not to do as we waded through the shocking carpet in reception.

"I'm alright now," he said. "I think it's wearing off."

"Remember," I said in his ear, "they don't know."

I wondered, as we stepped into the lift, if Miles had ever done anything more than drink and smoke a few spliffs.

"If you see something that looks ... surprising, it's just the drugs," I said. "Don't say anything, alright?"

"Like what?" he said.

"Well, it's hard to say. Just keep it to a minimum."

We walked down the corridor to Dr Johnson's

room. It was going well.

"Michael will be here," Miles said.

Shit. I'd forgotten about that. I'd been planning a quick in and out, Angus style.

"And Helen. And Mum."

"Great. Well, just remember. They don't know."

"And Matthew. And Heather."

"What's your mother called?" I asked him. We were outside Dr Johnson's room.

"Heidi," he said.

"Heidi?" I opened the door.

Heidi looked up at me from her chair by Dr Johnson's bed. It was the worst name anyone could have chosen for her. She was sort of grizzled … but all over, like someone had drawn her with a scratchy nib. I smiled at her anyway. Then I looked around the room, still smiling, at the other Johnsons.

You know how it is with some people when you first meet them: you just know you're going to like them. The Johnsons were the opposite of that. I don't think they'd been talking before I opened the door. They weren't talking after either, but in a much more hostile way. As a family, they bristled.

"You're late," one of the brothers said.

"Yes," Miles said.

Good. A short, simple answer.

"Have you had an accident?" a sister said, looking at the unfortunate spread of Bolognese sauce.

"No. I had something to eat," Miles said.

Good. This was alright. He positioned himself by his mother's chair. The siblings adjusted their spacings to make room for him, a nice even spread of Johnsons. I wondered if they ever touched each other. As an honorary member of the clan I thought I was entitled to know. I held out my hand to brother No.2, because he was nearest and because I wanted to piss him off. I wanted to piss them all off for being so fucking pissy.

"I don't think now is the time for introductions," he said.

Dr Johnson gurgled. This could be it ... but then he carried on sucking in, wheezing out, sucking in, wheezing out ... not sucking in. Everyone stopped breathing with him. You couldn't help it. Was it all over? No, there he went again.

Breathing resumed, hostile brother No.1 glared at me with his piggy eyes, just in case I hadn't realised yet that I was unwanted, unwelcome, to be held responsible for Miles' dilapidation and that I should wait outside. Yes, he said it all with the one look. I moved back to the door but I stayed in the room.

"We'd prefer it if you'd leave," he said.

How did he know? He hadn't checked with the others. Dr Johnson gurgled again. I took this as a sign that he wanted me to stay.

"I am very fond of your father," I said.

"Who are you, though?" the other sister said.

"I'm an old friend of Miles'," I said. "His oldest friend." It was worth a punt. There was every chance they wouldn't know and really I had to stay. I couldn't leave Miles in a room with these people, not even on a good day. "Even older than Harry," I said.

I smiled at her. Yup, even older than that.

"Who's Harry?" she said.

I carried on smiling. See? my smile was saying. I know more about your brother than you do. Heidi shuffled slightly in her chair, to let us know we were disrupting Her Boniness. She made Jessica look well-nourished. But the sister wanted to know.

"Who's Harry?" she asked Miles.

"My second oldest friend," he said.

Good boy. He put his hand on the back of his mother's chair. She waved a scraggy claw at him, to let him know he was too close. Or too bothersome. Or too ... whatever. Then we lapsed into more hostile silence.

I don't like my own family.

I liked the Johnsons even less. They were vile people. I thought that maybe Dr Johnson knew this too because at this point he opened his eyes, looked right at me and said, "Hallo, my boy." Suddenly I had credibility.

"Hallo, Sir," I said.

This went down well with Heidi and the brothers. Maybe they'd got me wrong ...

They fell back into their customary hostile silence while they thought it over.

"So," I said as soon as I could, because really we were pushing our luck staying any longer. "Time's getting on, Miles."

"Sorry?" brother No.1 said.

Miles said nothing. He was staring at a print on

the wall.

"We've got a gig later," I said.

"A gig? Miles isn't going to go gallivanting round London tonight."

"Well, we've got a gig," I said. "It's important."

"More important than this?" brother No.1 snorted.

"He can't possibly," a sister said. "Can he, Mum?"

"We said we were all going to stay," other sister said.

"Be together as a family," first sister said.

Shame you left it so long, I thought, but I said: "Why don't you ask Miles what he wants to do?"

"Miles?" second sister said. "Miles ... "

But Miles was miles away, frowning at the print. It was a cheerful kind of picture, a sandy beach with sailing boats out to sea and children playing in the waves. But it was still fine. He could be doing a dignified silence.

"I don't think Miles wants to lower himself to answer," I said. Which covered it pretty well, I thought.

"Oh, for God's sake," brother No.1 said. "I think it's about time you left."

"He has got a point," brother No.2 said. "It is up to Miles. I was going to go along myself later, for an hour or so."

So that was Michael.

"And this could take days," I said, meaning it was impossible to say and were they all going to

58

stand around in Dr Johnson's room with no sleep and no jobs to go to until the old man croaked? But they took it to mean that I had a problem fitting Dr Johnson's death into my diary. Which I did, but they didn't know that. "Tragically," I added. No, that was worse, worse, worse. They all glared at me, except Miles. And Heidi, who might actually be closer to death than Dr Johnson. Or dead already. No, she twitched.

"I want you to leave now," brother No.1 said, whatever his name was. "Miles is staying here with us." He took a step towards me. I tried to take a step backwards but the door was in the way. And to open it I was going to have to take a step towards him. Or two. Um ...

"How do they do that?" Miles said.

"What?" the Johnsons said, including Heidi. But not Dr Johnson, of course.

"It's amazing," he said. "Look. Look at the water in the picture. It's actually moving. It really is. Look, everyone, the boats are actually moving. Isn't it great?"

Everyone looked at the picture. Then they looked at me, including Miles. Um ...

"Isn't it amazing?" he burbled happily. "I'm not tripping, I swear," he said to whoever was still listening.

"What have you done to Miles?" the sisters wailed.

"Get out," brother No.1 snarled at me. He was much too close.

"And I want to tell you that I love you all," Miles said. "Before Dad dies. I want you to know that I really, really love you and that ... " You know how it goes.

The sisters were ashen now, touching fingertips but only just in a gesture of support at this final outrage, the final straw, the final breach of the family code, perhaps. Heidi was in a coma of embarrassment. Or was she dead? No, she blinked. Brother No.1 went red all over ... no, cerise ... no, purple ... while I wondered if, in some tragic twist of fate, he was about to pre-decease his almost dead parents and possibly take me with him ... and then Michael grabbed him and pulled him away.

"I think you'd really better go," he said. "Take Miles with you. I'll catch up later."

I grabbed Miles and dragged him out of the room.

"I love you, Mum. I love you, Dad," he was shouting. "I'll come back later. I love you ... " etc. etc. "What's the matter?" he said as I bundled him into the lift. "Are we late or something? I only wanted to tell them I love them."

I gave him a little hug. What can you say?

"Thank you for coming with me," he gushed. "Thank you for staying. You're more like a brother to me than ... " Than what? Than his brothers? Than a euphonium?

But I'd lost him. He flung himself on me and hung on in a full embrace. Sweet. I checked the time over his shoulder. Not bad: seventeen minutes, a long seventeen minutes, certainly, but we were still on schedule.

8

Electra was sitting at the kitchen table when we got home. She'd opened a bottle of wine. There were two glasses on the table ready, I supposed, for me and her. I parked Miles by the dresser.

"What have you done to him?" she said.

"Why does everyone think it's my fault?" I said.

He was looking at a blue and white vase that Jessica puts pens and stuff in.

"I'm just trying to get this pattern," he said. "Why is everything moving?"

"You're a bit loved up, Miles," I said. "I'm going to make you better."

"I don't want to be made better," he said. "I am better."

I heard someone upstairs in the back bathroom, trying to flush the lav.

"Who's that?" I said.

"Kate," Electra said.

"Kate?"

"Kate Kennedy. Sally's daughter."

"Fucking hell, Electra. What did you bring her round here for?"

"For a quiet drink before the gig. She's really upset."

"She's coming to the gig? Isn't she a bit ... young?"

"She's eighteen," Electra said. "Like me."

"For fuck's sake," I said.

"I didn't know you were going to get her father completely trashed."

"He's not her father. And why does everyone think it's my fault? Is that the Chateau Lafite?"

She checked the label.

"Yes."

"For fuck's sake, Electra."

"What's the matter now? It's just a bottle of wine."

I could hear Kate yanking on the chain upstairs ... clankety ... clankety ... she'd done it. The water flushed through the amusingly original plumbing. Miles was holding his head sideways to get a better look at the vase.

"It's amazing," he said. "It come and goes ... je vais et je vien ... "

"How's he going to do the gig like that?" Electra said.

"He'll be alright. It's hours to go yet."

"Er ... like three hours?"

"He'll be fine. I have a plan."

I could hear Kate coming downstairs. Miles was holding onto the dresser with both hands. His head was upside down now. He was swaying in time to the pattern. Or something.

"I don't think Kate should see him like this," Electra said. "It'll destroy her world."

She looked at me. I detected a hint of dissent behind her baby eyes. Aha. The beginning of the end, then.

"For fuck's sake," I said.

But still ... what to do? I needed no further complications in what had turned out to be a complicated day.

"Let's go outside and look at the roses," I said to Miles. "They're amazing too."

I helped him get upright, which kind of involved holding his head ... so when he was upright and the room had sorted itself out, which took a while, I was still holding his head. But then he returned the gesture, putting both his hands irresistibly ... believe me, I tried ... on either side of my head and kissing me full on my mouth. I'd been trying to say, Miles, please don't, so it was easy enough for him to slip his tongue in there.

Kate came in just then. I'd never seen her before: if Sid Vicious had ever put on three stone to play for the school hockey team, that's what he would've looked like ... or she. Anyway, she started screaming in short little yelps. I'd no idea she was such a conservative girl. I tried to signal that it was just a friendly sort of kiss while Electra tried to reassure her, distract her, get her out of the room ... anything would have done. Miles came up for air.

"I think it's time for your bath now," I said. He allowed me to lead him away. I think he was as shocked as I was. But not as shocked as Kate. She was sobbing as I steered him upstairs ... it's disgusting, how could he the bastard etc. etc. which was possibly a bit rich, coming from her.

But not to worry. A tepid bath and a gallon of orange juice later and Miles was fighting fit. I called Angus to ask for clues while he dried himself and put on some clean clothes.

"The white ones," he said. "That's what you want. I might come to the gig later."

I assumed he was suffering from hallucinatory sociophilic delusions, which he easily could have even though I'd just made it up. If he'd been anywhere near the gear Miles had ingested ...

"Yeah, great," I said. "See you later."

I sat on the bedroom floor and unwrapped Jessica's order. I was being extra careful now. I peeled the mulch apart into colour coded wraps: white for coke, swirly psychedelic for swirly psycho effects and a fetching deep blue for deep, deep sleep. I looked at the blue wraps. They were intact. I looked at Miles, buttoning up one of my rather lovely shirts.

Did we really need a trombone player so badly? Should I be thinking differently? But he was so pathetic I couldn't do it to him. And the band was going out as The Jimmy Edwards Experience. Without a trombone, the name was just obliquely stupid.

"How are you, Miles?" I said.

"Great. Look. I'm sorry about what happened earlier."

"Which bit?"

He frowned, genuinely puzzled. There was only

one bit?

"At the hospital. My family. It was your hat. You didn't take it off."

"Right. My hat. But apart from that everything's square?"

"Yeah, of course." He tucked my rather lovely shirt into another pair of my genuine vintage trousers. "Have you got any braces?" he said. "We should all wear braces."

Oh clueless child. I smiled nicely before demolishing the braces idea. He'd be suggesting bow ties next.

"I'm just going to have a shower," I said. "Are you alright to get the van?"

"What van?"

"The van we take the gear to the gig in. The white van."

"That's not my van. That's Sally's van."

"Well, can you go and get it?"

There was a sticky silence.

"Well, no," Miles said. "She won't lend it to me now."

"So how are we going to get the gear to the gig?"

"I've only got a trombone," Miles said. "I can carry it."

But I couldn't carry my Hammond organ, amplifier, PA system, mic stands etc. Fuck.

"Oh," I said. "Where is your trombone?"

"Downstairs. Sally threw it out of the window this morning, after my wallet and my phone. It was in its case," he added, to let me know she wasn't a total

66

bitch.

"Right." Shit. "Er ... O.K." Shit, shit, shit. "Um ... well, the first thing to do is have some of this." I think I meant the only thing. "Then the ideas will start flowing." With luck. I unwrapped a white wrap. "Just lick a finger and dip it in."

"More drugs?" Miles was horrified. "I'm only just coming round from the last lot."

"This is different," I said. "It'll sharpen you up. Believe me, Miles you need it."

And as things were turning out, so did I.

We did look good, I had to admit. We looked good anyway but with a dab of coke spangle adjusting my vision ...

"You're a handsome man, aren't you?" Miles said, like he'd only just realised.

"Yes. But please don't kiss me again."

"What?"

"Nothing. Come on." We were still hanging around in the bedroom, standing side by side in front of the mirror. "We've got to get going."

"No problem," Miles said. "This room's such a great colour."

"Yeah." We were in the passage now.

"So's this," he said, running his hand along the wall. "Jessica's got great taste, hasn't she? I only just realised."

We stood on the landing, looking down the staircase into the hall below us. I've never liked Jessica's style ... she tries much, much too hard to look like she hasn't tried at all ... but suddenly the whole thing worked. It was the coke. Hers was a house for coke-heads. With coke, you didn't notice what a phony little piece of pretentious shit she really was. But I'd have to think about this later. Right now I had a burglary to commit.

We stood on the pavement and rang the bell for Sally's flat. Then we knocked. She lived above a flower shop. I knew she wouldn't be in. No-one ever is in when they've just split up from their boyfriend. They go out and have a great time with the friends you hated, out of spite.

"She won't lend us the van even if she answers the door," Miles said. "You don't know her like I do."

"She might, for old times' sake," I said. "Has she got a job tonight?"

"No. But she won't. She's not in anyway. We're going to have to think of something else."

"There isn't time for anything else. What's round the back?"

"We can't break in," Miles said.

"We can. We've come this far. We have to do the gig. We can't do the gig without the van."

"Well, no."

"Where is the van?"

"Round the back."

"So what are we waiting for?"

We went round the back.

"It looks easy enough," I said. I was standing on the roof of the van looking over the back wall. There was a fire escape up the back of the building. "You can say you lost your keys."

"To Sally?" Miles said. "She knows I haven't got any keys."

"No, to the police. It's perfectly legit to break into your own place. We can't waste any more time. I'll give you a leg over the wall."

"What?"

"I'm joking." I jumped down. It was further than I thought. I reminded myself of the optimism of cocaine. Time for another dab, then. I gave one to Miles as well. "Think of it as getting to know Jessica better," I said.

Miles bunked me up onto the wall. It wasn't high: six and a half feet maybe, a big eighteen hands, but it was harder than it sounds, mainly because by now we were laughing like idiots. I didn't jump this time. I scrabbled down the inside of the door ... easy ... and I was across the yard and up the fire escape and things were going well. I tried Sally's kitchen door, just in case. She didn't look like the kind of girl who would forget to lock her flat but you can get lucky ... not tonight. I checked the windows: all shut ... except for one on the second floor, a bedroom or bathroom. I'm going to have to go on up, I mimed at Miles. He was on the roof of the van. He gave me a big thumbs up. Fine.

The window on the second floor was on a catch. I knocked it up, snaked an arm in and managed to get the big one undone. I climbed through ... easy peasy ... into a bedroom: Kate's bedroom, I guessed. It smelt of ... sporting socks. I opened the door. There was music on downstairs. Still, we'd rung. And knocked. Loads of people leave music on when they go out, and lights and TVs and grills and whatever else.

I sneaked on downstairs in the dark. There was a lot of woodchip in this flat. I could feel the bumps under my fingers. Now I was in a hall. I took my bearings. The kitchen had to be ... that one. Bingo. It smelt of ... basil. I unlocked the back door and stepped out onto the fire escape. Miles was ecstatic.

"Where does she keep the keys?" I hissed down at him.

"On a hook by the front door," he hissed back. "It's the ones with a leather fob."

Fob? What kind of word was that? But the real bummer was having to find the front door. I had no idea how the rest of the flat was laid out apart from badly, so badly it showed in the dark. I could risk a light ... no. That would be taking the piss.

The music was coming from a door on my right: the sitting room then. A line of light was leaking out onto the hall carpet. I tried the door next to it: a walk-in cupboard. I tried one across the hall: another cupboard, for fuck's sake. There were only two left. I wasn't thinking I'd find anything much behind either of them. I just wanted to find the keys and get out of there but what I found instead was Sally in the bath with the asparagus grower and a bottle of Cava ... how cheap is that? ... and candles everywhere. She did a little scream. He tried to hide behind the shower curtain.

"Alright, Sal?" I said. She didn't say anything. "Can I take the van on?"

She nodded. And she said with her cheating eyes, please don't tell Miles. Please, please, though why she should care what I told him I didn't get straight away. I waited for a while, leaning up against the door frame, but they didn't offer me a drink so I said:

"Well, we're running late, what with all the hospital visits to Miles' dying father to fit in. I'd better get going. See you later."

I shut the door and left her with her cheapskate squeeze. I opened the only door left to try. It was another cupboard, crammed with cooking stuff. There was nothing for it. I had to go back. This time I knocked.

"Sorry to bust in again," I said, "but I can't find the front door."

"It's through the sitting room," Sally said. She wanted to kill me. Too bad. I might have broken into her flat but there was nothing she could say and she knew it. I fetched the keys and snuck out the back way, pretending for Miles' sake that we were still playing burglars.

"That was so cool," he said when we were in the van. "I would never dare do anything like that." I shrugged and lit a cigarette. I was thinking what a cow Sally had turned out to be, not because of her cheating heart but because she was a moral highground sort of girl and I hate that. If you set yourself up as the well-behaved one you'd better stick to it, or else.

I wound down my window and blew the smoke away from Miles.

"Sally's going to go nuts when she finds out," he said. "I like cocaine. Can I have some more, please?"

"In a while," I said. I took a big lungful of smoke.

"Can I have a cigarette instead?"

"No," I said, and then he tapped me on the shoulder, like he was trying to draw my attention to something but when I turned my head to see what he planted his gob firmly over mine. I have to admit, his timing was great. I had to breathe out.

"Miles, you've got to stop kissing me," I said when we broke. "Even if it's just for the smoke. I feel used. And people will talk. We have our reputations to think of."

9

We were sitting at the bar in Louis' Place by 10:28, waiting for the rest of the band to turn up. The gear was on the stage, the van was parked, our pints were slipping down like nectar ... we were superhumans. Or at least I was. I wasn't so sure about Miles. It was getting to me now. No-one could be so desperate for nicotine they'd go in to bat for the opposing team. It had to be the stress of his father dying. It was affecting his hormones.

"It's the power of positive thought," I said, saluting him with my pint. He was shredding a beer mat. "We believed, and against all the odds we did it."

"Are you trying to tell me I can give up smoking if I really want to?"

"No," I said, because I wasn't. "I'm talking about ..."

"Because I know that," he butted in. "The thing is, do I really want to?"

I looked at Miles, sitting on his bar stool. I looked at the pile of shredded beer mat. I tried to recall where we were up to with this ... and failed. I also tried to recall why I cared so much ... no, I couldn't remember that either.

"D'you know what?" I said. "Suddenly I don't give a shit. Have a fag if you want."

He was just thinking about reaching across me to take one from my packet of Camels when his mobile rang. It was Michael, telling him that Dr Johnson was hanging in there but that he should get back straight after the gig.

"I've changed my mind," he said.

"Good. The first day's the worst. It can only get easier."

"But look what's happened," Miles said.

"That's not giving up the fags. That's just ... " But I couldn't think of anything. "Here's the Steves and Eddie," I said, to distract him.

I was glad to see the band had made an effort. They looked dead cool in their linen suits and real shoes. We just needed Luke now.

"So what happened to you two?" Eddie said. He was tapping his drumsticks against the plush upholstery on a bar stool. Little clouds of dust puffed out at every thwack.

"You wouldn't believe me if I told you," I said.

"Try me," he said. This was wrong. This was hostile talk. The Steves had lined up behind him.

"Where were you then?" Steve the bass said. He was from Birmingham. He liked hitting people. I could tell he wanted to hit me now.

"We're fucking pissed off with you not showing up," Steve the guitar said.

What? Miles was no help. He was on his third beer mat.

"The rehearsal, you twat," Steve the bass said.

74

"We fucking waited for over an hour."

The rehearsal. Right. I'd completely forgotten. How could I have forgotten?

"Look ... " I said, but before I could get going Eddie said:

"You told us to dress up for this gig. We've been all over fucking London looking for these suits."

"And very lovely you look too," I said.

"So what happened to you two?" he said. We were back at the beginning. I hadn't enjoyed the conversation the first time. I didn't want to do it again. I made a face to indicate that I didn't quite get the question.

"You look like shit," Steve the bass said. Which was helpful, at least. I checked out Miles. I checked out me. I rubbed my eyes. He was right. Somehow I'd failed to notice that we did actually look like shit. Our suits were ... shit. Filthy. But then we had climbed onto Sally's van and I'd scaled a wall and Miles had clearly ... now I was looking ... had a little lie down in a puddle. I was about to agree that he was right, that we did indeed look like shit but it was too late. They thought I was taking the piss.

"That's it," Eddie said. "We've had enough. And what the fuck have you done to Miles?"

"Why does everyone think it's my fault?" I said. "Look. His father's dying and he's given up smoking and Sally's thrown him out. And he met Jessica." This would surely explain everything. Eddie knew Jessica intimately ... but there was still no sign of forgiveness on his ugly face. He'd crossed his arms.

75

His biceps were bulging through the sleeves of his jacket. His drumsticks looked like a weapon. "It's been a heavy day," I ploughed on. Louis Armstrong was watching me from his tastefully framed black and white photo behind the bar. He wasn't buying it either. "I really am sorry about the rehearsal," I said, keeping my voice level, reasonable. "I swear it won't happen again. I'll even pay for your suits if you want ... Eddie? Don't leave. Steve ... Steve ... come on guys. I'll make it up to you, I promise ... "

"Aren't you going to go after them?" Miles said.

"No. Fuck it. Who needs a drummer? Or a bass player. And Steve's a pretty shit guitarist anyway. We'll do the gig as the stripped down Jimmy Edwards Experience: piano, trombone and trumpet. We'll take our trousers off and do it in our underpants."

"Brilliant," Miles said. "Can I have some more cocaine, please?"

"When Luke gets here," I said.

We were on our third pint when Luke finally showed up. He looked even worse than we did.

"I've just been robbed," he said, "just up the road. I was getting out of my car and they jumped me and stole my trumpet. I chased them for fucking miles man, and I had them. I got it back but then the little bastards beat the crap out of me and stole it again. So I've just been robbed twice. Sorry I'm late."

"We're doomed," Miles said.

"Shut up, Miles," I said. "You need some ice on that eye. Mike? Over here a minute."

Luke's front teeth were bloody. He wanted me to test them.

"I can't do it myself," he said. "I'm a total baby when it's teeth."

"We are doomed," Miles said.

"Shut up, Miles," I said. "You should leave them," I told Luke. "Even if they are loose they can grow back in."

"You can't play the trumpet without teeth," Luke said.

"You can't play the trumpet without a trumpet," I said.

"That's true as well," he said. He always was the most reasonable trumpet player I knew.

"You're bleeding from your ear," I told him. "How hard did they hit you?"

"But we are doomed," Miles said. "This whole gig is doomed."

"Shut up, Miles," Luke said. "Not that hard. They were only little runts. D'you think I've got brain damage?"

"No," I said. "Of course not." Although it would be difficult to tell. I suspected that Luke had already taken one punch too many. For such an easy sort of man he got into a lot of fights. Mike had fetched some ice wrapped in a tea towel. We took Luke out to the Gents and cleaned him up. Miles was good at this. He sat him on a chair and fussed around, all nursey. It seemed to bring him out of himself. He tried cleaning up our jackets as well. He loved it. I wondered if he was going to make a start on the urinals.

"But what are you going to do?" Luke said. "You've got no trumpet now."

"We've got no bass or drums either," I said. "Or guitar."

"So where is everyone?"

"They're dead. I can't say I'm sorry. You can play the drums, can't you?"

"Like her out of White Stripes, yeah."

"Mike's got an old kit in the cellar somewhere. Have some of this," I pulled a wrap out of my inside pocket, "and we're sorted."

"That's not like you," Luke said. "What's going on?"

"You wouldn't believe me if I told you," I said, and being a reasonable, easy sort of man he was happy with that.

There were a few moments left for reflection before we went on stage. We were in the Gents, waiting to strip for our dramatic entrance. Miles Davis was looking down from another tastefully framed black and white photograph above the row of basins. He was clearly more sympathetic than Louis, being an unreliable lunatic junky himself. Not that we were in his league, God forbid, but if I was honest with myself the coke had been a bad idea. It was too late now, of course. We were committed. We'd started so we had to finish.

"You alright, mate?" Luke said.

"Yeah. I just started to slide a bit there." I reached

into my inside pocket.

"More?" he said. "Are you sure?"

"It's got to be done," I said. "We've gone too far. There's no way back from where we are."

It was true. And it rhymed. But we were fine. We were focused. We were here and we had a plan to save the gig, the band, the tour. And half the band meant twice as much money so in the end it was a blessing, all of it.

"You ready?" I asked Luke. He nodded. "No matter what, just keep it going. Miles? If you can't remember the dance routine, make it up. Keep moving. Swing that trombone. O.K. boys, trousers off."

The place was packed, which was a good start, and the no-trousers got a laugh. Electra was at a table with a bunch of her girlfriends. Michael was near the front. The bar was heaving and I thought I saw Angus right at the back by the door, talking to … it had to be the man from Ersatz Promotions. I took all this in as I gave the whole place my biggest, cutest smile.

"Welcome to The Jimmy Edwards Experience … stripped down," I said. Another laugh: the people who knew the band understood the joke, the people who didn't laughed anyway. I sat down at my piano and arranged my shirt to cover my underpants. Another laugh.

Miles was ready, grinning with his trombone.

Luke was ready, twinkling from behind Mike's

drum kit.

I was ready … and a one … a two … a one, two, three, four …

We were off, a little boogie-woogie opener to get their feet tapping. And it sounded alright, edgy and a bit rough but in a good way. Luke was beating the crap out of the kit. Miles was blowing and honking and sliding and dancing. The audience were looking … interested. This was something different, something other than the usual well-polished jazz standards. I should've thought of it ages ago. The band had been reinvented. I caught Miles' eye, to let him know we were on the last verse. I gave Luke a nod … brilliant. We finished tight as the dog's bollocks.

I kept the first set short. The audience cheered us off the stage. So far, so good.

We re-grouped in the Gents. Someone had taken our trousers.

"It'll be Mike," I said. "He's put them somewhere safe."

I could tell Luke and Miles thought they'd been stolen. I was suddenly well pissed off with being the cheerful, coping one in our group. That was usually Miles' job. Still, only another hour or so to go.

"Who'd want to steal three pairs of trousers?" I said. They weren't convinced.

"Some bastard would," Luke said. Despite the ice, his left eye had nearly closed. "People will steal anything."

"They were nice trousers," Miles said, as if this latest setback could push him over the edge of reason.

"They were my trousers," I pointed out.

"My trousers weren't your trousers," Luke said.

"Look. Never mind about the trousers. The gig's going well. The audience love us." I reached into my inside pocket. "Have some more of this and everything will be fine."

"I don't want any more," Luke said. "I feel like shit."

"So you have some more and you'll feel better," I said. "It's only to get us through the gig."

"I don't want any more either," Miles said. "My life is on a downwards spiral, spinning out of control into an abyss of disease and total destruction."

I wished, not for the first time that day, that I'd paid more attention to Jessica's drug habit. Cocaine made you happy, didn't it? Or was that a myth put about by the drug cartels in Colombia? It had always made me happy. But then I'd always been happy before I'd taken any because I'd always been pissed at a party somewhere. So maybe it didn't make you happy. I assessed my own mental state. I wasn't that happy, I had to admit. But clearly the solution was to do more, and do it properly. We needed lines, big, fat lines through rolled up twenties like proper coke users.

"Let's go in the cubicle," I said. "If we're going to be famous jazz musicians we have to learn to handle our drugs,"

"But you're already a total pisshead," Luke said.

"So I need to broaden my experience. Alcohol is my drug of choice. Think of this," I waved a wrap at him, "as our introduction to a whole new life."

My argument was persuasive. Three minutes later we were fine ... Really Fine.

"Woo," Miles said. "Better."

"Good," I said. I was texting Electra. We needed beer but we couldn't risk mingling with our fans. It would spoil the show.

"We should go out, before someone comes in," Luke said.

It seemed a shame to leave the lavatory. I'd grown fond of it. But there was the gig, and the pints arriving, and later trousers to be found ...

I opened the door and we jostled out, laughing, lit up, boys in underpants. Angus was having a piss in the urinal. He was in drag. It kind of suited him. He looked like Jack Lemon. Michael was leaning against the row of basins. They glanced at each other ... and because my brain was now working beyond the speed of light I knew sooner than instantly that they knew each other. Somehow they knew each other.

"Well, hiya doodie boys," I said. It had to be completely obvious that I was totally off my tits, at least to Angus. He was looking at Michael. O.K. Somehow it was obvious to Michael as well.

"That was an interesting performance," Michael said.

"And there's more where that came from," I

sparkled, "much, much more. Do you two need introducing or are you already bosom buddies?" I wasn't sure why I was talking like this, apart from the fact that I'd lost control of my mouth. "You seen any trousers anywhere? Here's Electra with our pints. Do you know Electra? Electra, this is Michael. Michael, Electra. And this is Luke. And for those of you who don't know him already, this is Angus." I beamed. I smoothed my hair in the mirror above the row of basins. I straightened my shirt. I straightened my eyebrows with a wet finger.

Everything was great. Everything was fine. We were all wonderful people. The gig was going to go down in history as the beginning, The Beginning of Everything. It was so exciting I had to do a little tap dance …

Miles caught my eye from his tasteful frame above the row of basins. Now that's more like it, he was saying. I knew he was right. I'd arrived.

10

But where had I arrived?

I was awake but my eyes were shut. If I opened them I would discover who was next to me in bed. There was definitely someone else. It wasn't Electra. The smell was wrong. And I needed to find out whose bed I was in.

Very, very slowly then. I opened one eye. It was a man. Oh Jesus Mary no no no. I tried to leap out of the bed … my bed at least … but it didn't work. I got as far as lifting my head off the pillow. God I felt ill.

"Good morning," Angus said.

"What the fuck are you doing here?" I said.

"I've been watching you sleep."

No no no. And no.

"Why?" It was all I could manage. I seriously had to pull myself together. I needed to know much, much more than that, like "What's the time?" and "Where's Miles?" The effort nearly killed me.

"It's just after six. Miles is downstairs," Angus said. He took a pull on a huge spliff and offered it to me. I threw up over the side of the bed. It was the thought of it … the thought of ever sucking scorching, poisonous smoke into my terrified lungs, the thought of ever drinking anything other than pure, clear mountain water, the thought of ever eating anything other than crisp green leaves ever, ever again …

"I'll take that as a no," Angus said. I could hear him stubbing out the spliff, out of respect for my near-death status. And it was my bedroom. I would institute a strict no smoking policy as soon as I could say anything that complicated.

"What happened?" I said next, after a bit of a lull. I'd found some water … no, it was vodka. I threw up again.

"When?" he said.

"Last night."

"When last night?"

Let's start at the beginning. That way the end might make more sense.

"At the gig," I said. I couldn't remember the second set. I tried harder. It still wasn't there.

"I can show you if you want," Angus said. "I filmed some of it on my mobile."

He held the little screen in front of my face. I was on my feet, playing my piano with one hand, gyrating my hips and swinging my shirt around my head like a lasso. It was quite an achievement really. We panned to Miles. He was dancing a keepy-uppy sort of dance but without the football and he was blowing so hard he looked like his head was going to explode. We panned to Luke, who appeared to be in the middle of a monster rock-style solo, a tribute to Cozi Powell, perhaps.

"What tune were we playing?" I asked Angus.

"I think it was Great Balls of Fire," he said. "Well, you were. I don't know about the others."

That wasn't on the set list. It wasn't anywhere near it. We panned to the audience. They were laughing. Some of them were dancing. Electra's face loomed into the picture. She was crying, pushing her way through to the Ladies.

"Why's Electra crying?" I said.

"Her mother had just turned up. She had to go to Harrogate and when she got back her husband had gone. Vamoosed. He left a note."

"Shit." Poor Electra. Poor Electra's Mum. That was two break-ups in one weekend. There was bound to be a third. There always is. "So why is she downstairs?" I said.

"You dumped her."

"Did I? I didn't mean to." Or maybe I did. "How did she take it?"

"She was fine. She's with Miles now."

"Miles?"

"Yeah. After the fight you invited everyone back here for a party. They got it together then."

"Who's everyone?"

"How many people do you know? Double it. It was a great party."

"Jesus. I'm too fucked to think about all this."

"Yeah."

"So … why are you in my bed?"

"There was nowhere else to go."

"How about home?" I suggested, not unreasonably. "What fight?"

"That's the whole point," Angus said. "I can't go home, can I? The bastards have been watching me for weeks. If they'd caught me on my own … "

"Which is why you came to the drag. The gig." Now I was remembering. God, I must have been in orbit. Angus in a frock had seemed as sensible as Angus in a suit, Angus in Levis, Angus incontrovertible …

"Yeah. I had to get out of the flat without them spotting me. But they've got contacts everywhere. They found me anyway and they would've had me if Luke and Michael hadn't been there. I owe your drummer. He's the best scrapper I've ever seen."

"Michael. Who's Michael?"

"An old friend of mine. Your mate's brother."

"So where are they now?"

"Luke had to go to hospital and Michael's been arrested. Luke's been arrested too but he needed stitches."

"No, not them," I said. I might have found the energy to snap. "The others. The ones who've been watching you." I was thinking, of course, that they could bust in at any moment. I was thinking more drug cartels, crazy Colombians, vicious Venezuelans, turf wars, midnight planes landing in Essex …

"The Welsh." He said this with such dread I wasn't sure I'd heard him right.

"Who?"

"The Welsh. They're not in Wales any more. They're muscling in all over London. They've given up on the Valleys and they're over the border

… Manchester, Leeds, even fucking Liverpool. It's all Maggie's fault, the bastard bitch. She should've kept the mines open. Now look what's happened. They're tough, I'm telling you."

"But where are they?" I wanted him to be more specific, like Fulham or Wimbledon. Or the nick, with luck. "What do they want?"

"They're everywhere," he said, "and they want everything. They want my clients, they want my patch, they even want my fucking flat. They've got it, as it happens. All of it. Do you think Jessica would mind if I stayed a few weeks?"

"Sure," I said. "Stay as long as you like." I liked Angus better now that I was in bed with him. He seemed more approachable somehow, less of a paranoid lunatic psycho. And if the Welsh already had everything they wanted there was a good chance they'd leave him alone. "Did you get any sleep?" I said.

"Sleep?" he said. "I don't sleep. I smoke."

That was it then. He relit his enormous spliff. I decided to let it go for now. I had to get up anyway.

There were other things I should've asked Angus. I realised this as soon as I got to the top of the stairs, things like, of all the people I know doubled, how many stayed over? And were there any fatalities? Things like that. It would've prepared me for the carnage.

God. It was a depressing sight.

I wanted to leave and come back when someone

had cleared up. I didn't want this mess. So I stood at the top of the stairs and considered simply leaving: leaving the house, the band, Miles, Jessica ... and now Angus as well. I needed clean clothes and my passport. I would go to see my mother in Ireland. That's how desperate I was.

But to get clean clothes I would have to go back to my bedroom and somehow I couldn't face it. I didn't want to be mixing with people who smoked huge spliffs at 6:13am and never slept. It was all so disgustingly bad for my health. Right now, right at this moment, I wanted to be with people who went to bed early and drank enough water.

Then the doorbell rang. How had the doorbell rung?

No. Wrong question. What mattered was Why? Everyone I knew doubled was either here or had been here until very recently. Why come back when you're only going to get involved in the clearing up process? What kind of idiot would do that?

I stood at the top of the stairs, waiting for them to go away.

Then it occurred to me that it could be the Welsh, looking to finish Angus ... although it seemed unlikely they would ring the bell. And anyway, the front door was open. There was a leg keeping it open ... but then they could be the sick and twisted kind of mobster, the kind who make a point of being very polite as they tear out your toe nails with a pair of mole-grips, the kind who wear spectacles stuck together with Elastoplast and tank tops knitted by their mums.

Very slowly, the door pushed open.

I thought about running. I could still make it out through the kitchen if I was very, very quick. But who was I kidding? I could barely walk. Better to stand and face it than try to run and be hunted down. I thought suddenly of a mangy fox the hounds had killed right in front of me as it tried to double back and ran smack into them …

"Hallo?" the door pusher said. "Can I come in?" The owner of the voice blundered over the body in the porch and into the hall. Jesus. It was Sally's mate, the asparagus grower. He looked around and then squinted up at me, standing at the top of the stairs. "Hallo?" he said. He didn't sound too sure. "I believe my wife and daughter are here."

He hadn't recognised me. But then why would he? We'd never been formally introduced.

"Can I come in?" He took another step into the carnage.

"You are in."

"Right. Can I look for them?"

"Do what you want." I started down the stairs.

"Right. Good. Thanks." He bent over the nearest sprawling body, peering to see who it might be, a hag in reverse drag picking over the corpses after a bloody battle. I can recognise a member of what's left of my family from a hundred paces. It's an aversion thing, an early warning system.

"Don't you know what they look like?" I asked him.

"I've lost my glasses," he said. "There was a fight. I can't see without them."

I left him to it and headed for the kitchen. He followed me, treading on anything in the way, crunching toes, fingers, a box of Kentucky Fried Chicken under his blind feet. Ketchup squirted out like the bird had just been fatally crushed … Kentucky Live Chicken.

"Perhaps you know them," he said next.

"Yeah," I said. "Perhaps I do." I was wondering if it would be possible to make a pot of tea: the kitchen wasn't looking like the kind of room you would ever want to make food in. I moved over to the sink. It was too full. I couldn't fill the kettle without taking out some of the empty cans, empty bottles, broken glasses, chunks of chucked up chicken Korma …

As I put the kettle back down a goldfish caught my eye, swimming past the transparent stripe at the five cups level, enough for a pot of tea after all. A lucky escape then, for both of us. And why would it surprise me? My sister's dealer wore frocks, my kettle housed a goldfish.

"Elizabeth Taylor," the asparagus grower was saying.

"Yeah," I said. "I never got the kaftan thing."

So. My humour was returning. Nearly time for a fag.

"No," he said. "That's my wife's name."

How to convey to this idiot that I cared nothing for his wife and daughter? I had someone of my own to find.

"Miles?" I yelled. "Where the fuck are you?"

There was a brief, embarrassed silence and then a scuffling noise, a pathetic injured rat scraping.

"What's that?" my companion said. Now he had the look of a worried mole. It was a vermin morning.

I picked my way across the kitchen and opened the larder door. Miles and Electra were inside. They'd made a little nest for themselves with cushions and rugs and a candle in a beer bottle, like children playing house. Or doctors and nurses. They looked up at me from their bed of shame in between the empty shelves. It was so predictable it was pitiful. I could tell by Electra's scowl that it had not been a successful union, also predictable.

"We couldn't get out," Miles whispered. He was very pale. Looking at him I suddenly felt much, much better. "Some bastard pushed the door shut."

"But surely your parents told you never to hide in cupboards?" I said. He started shaking his head, I don't know why. Maybe his parents had never bothered to pass on this vital information. Then he stopped shaking his head. It hurt too much.

"What's the time?" he said. It was a reflex question, the kind of thing you say when your brain has nothing in it but pain.

"Around seven."

He tried to work this out: seven ... seven ... what could it mean?

"I think I've really fucked up," he said next. "This is all wrong. What am I doing here? Oh God, I feel ill. Oh God," this said with mounting horror, "my dad's dying, isn't he? I've got to get to the hospital. I bet he's dead by now."

"He might not be. You're only missing four or five hours." Or six? It was hard to say accurately. "Someone would've called you," I pointed out.

He fumbled for his phone amongst the cushions and rugs ...

"Fuck, fuck, I must've turned it off for the gig. What am I going to tell them?"

All these questions. How the fuck would I know? I seemed to be in charge somehow. My status had changed overnight, without my realising. I was responsible. Miles was looking to me for guidance. I was offering advice. How could this have happened? But then a lot of mysterious things had happened since sundown ...

"It is a bit tricky," I said, "but I'm sure we'll think of something. Michael isn't there either."

I said this to make him feel better, like he wasn't the only flaky bastard son, but it didn't work. It flicked the switch on his memory reel and the action replay started to roll. I don't know where he was up to but after only a few brief seconds of total recall he threw himself down into his cushions in a fit of self-loathing and darkest despair. I thought he was over-playing it. Apart from a nearly dead father this could be a bog standard Sunday morning.

"Look," I said, "you don't have time for this crap. Stand up. Pull yourself together. I'll ring for a cab. Electra, I'm putting you in charge of clearing up.

Get all the overnight guests to give you a hand. It's the least they can do."

Sally's mate had blundered over and was standing behind me as I said this. I thought Electra was about to tell me to fuck off and die ... but it wasn't me, for once. It was him. As soon as she realised who was looking over my shoulder she opened her mouth and this terrible noise came out, formless rage, I suppose, which kind of moulded itself eventually into recognisable words.

"I can't believe you'd do that," she screamed. "How could you do that to Mum? I just can't believe ... " etcetera.

You probably worked out that Mr Taylor was her father. I should have worked it out too but I'd been distracted by the Johnson crisis, and now that I was thinking about it I wasn't sure I'd ever known her full name. Not that it made any difference to the immediate plan. It actually helped because there was no way Miles could stay in such a confined space with such a loud noise going on. And there was no way Electra's father could do the outraged parent. He didn't have a moral leg to stand on.

We left them in the kitchen.

"But what am I going to do?" Miles said.

We were in the hall. He knew where he was but he still had all the pathos of a lost child.

"Turn your phone back on?" I said.

"I can't. I can't face listening to all their messages. I'm going to pretend I lost it."

He dropped his phone on the tiles and started

stamping on it. Now he had all the slappable status of a two-year-old throwing a tantrum ... so there it was: yesterday I'd turned into a grown-up because I had to look after him. It was all coming back to me, the strange sense of grown-upness, of being someone who cared. I adjusted my shoulders slightly, square to fit my new identity.

"I can't go to the hospital looking like this," he whined.

No, indeed. Poor little lamb. And anyway, it wasn't really sarong weather. But we had to move fast. If there was anything to be salvaged from this total fuck up we had to leave now. But I still wasn't ready to go back upstairs, not yet.

I looked around the hall. Disgusting. I walked into the sitting room. Horrible. I walked back across the hall to the dining room. Revolting ... but there were two guys cosied up on a sofa sweetly sleeping in each other's arms. They looked about the right size. They looked much cleaner than anyone else I'd seen so far that morning. I woke them up.

"This is an emergency," I said. "We have to take your clothes."

They told me to fuck off.

"Look," I said. "This is my house. You crashed my party and now you're asleep on my sofa in my dining room. Give me your clothes, you bastards."

We got dressed in the porch. Doorstop man tried to grab my ankles. He wanted a drink of water. Our cab pulled up outside the gate.

"Where's my prize?" he shouted after us.

What?

"The dance competition," Miles said. "You organised a dance competition. It was called Last Man Standing. We had to call an ambulance. Someone actually had a heart attack."

"I'm just going to fetch it now," I shouted back at the man on the floor of my sister's porch.

As we walked down the path towards the gate I suddenly felt terrible, like really terrible, which doesn't ever happen to me and I found myself thinking Please God, which also doesn't ever happen to me, please, please God, please let all these people be gone by the time I get home. And because it was Sunday, and because I was being kind to my friend, and because I was possibly about to start weeping for the first time in years, I thought maybe there was a chance. Maybe Electra and her parents would clear up the house, shoo everyone out and leave a Thank You card on the kitchen table with an arrangement of beautiful flowers from Columbia Road. Maybe Angus would take it upon himself to cook a fabulous roast dinner for his generous housemates. Maybe Dr Johnson would be sitting up in bed with a cup of tea. Maybe Michael would be laughing about his little escapade on the wrong side of the tracks.

Maybe Jessica would stay in rehab where she belonged. Maybe.

11

I knew Dr Johnson was going to die as soon as we got to the hospital. Of course he was going to die. What I mean is I knew it was going to be that morning, that hour. He'd done his hanging on. There was never going to be a miracle.

We'd done the gig and now we required the miracle, to get the tour. I'd blown it.

It seemed like a very long time since we'd trekked across the shocking blue carpet in reception: if electric chairs are ever painted, that's the colour they'll be. A lot of stuff had happened since yesterday but it was alright now. We were here and we were looking tidy in our gay professional party wear. I thought I brought a strong sense of heterosexuality to my silver Lycra-mix shirt and pinstriped hipsters. Miles looked like he'd just come out and wanted everyone to know: blowsy flowery cheesecloth tucked into butt-hugging pink flares. But we were here, which mattered more than anything ... to me too, which I still didn't get.

"Can we swop clothes?" he asked me. We were in the lift. A male nurse was smiling at him.

"No. There's no time. Your father won't care what you're wearing."

"Everyone else will."

"You've got to stop worrying about what your family think of you," I said. The male nurse was nodding. "Be who you are."

"Be proud," the male nurse said.

"Oh God," Miles said.

I suppose I'd been planning on reuniting Miles with his family and then ... I didn't know what. Go somewhere clean and healthy for a while, an isolation tank, perhaps. Whatever, I felt I'd done my duty. But there was no-one around at Dr Johnson's end of the corridor, no nurses, no Johnsons, apart from the man himself and Miles.

"I'll get going," I said, but Miles wanted me to stay. I pointed out that his family hated me. He said he didn't care and anyway they weren't there. "But they'll be back," I said.

We were standing just inside Dr Johnson's room. He was making his blocked vacuum cleaner noise. It sounded bad, much worse than yesterday.

"He's going to die, isn't he?" Miles said.

"Yes."

"You've known that all along."

"Well, yes."

"Please don't go." He moved over to his father's bed and picked up his hand. Dr Johnson opened one eye, just a slit. There was something very animal in this, sleeping dog, dreaming cat. Then he closed it again. More awful noises. I guessed it was a matter of minutes.

"I'd better try to find someone," I said. I didn't want to be in at the kill.

"Don't," Miles said. "Don't leave me on my own. Dad? Dad?" Dr Johnson stirred. The eye opened again. "I'm so sorry there's no-one here. I don't know where they are. I'm sure they'll be back soon."

Dr Johnson made a noise like a rutting stag.

"I think that's a no," I said.

He nodded his head, a tiny movement but clear.

"If you could just hang on," Miles said.

Dr Johnson did his no noise.

"I don't think he wants to," I said.

"But he must. He must be with Mum at the ... " He couldn't say end, although it obviously was.

Another no noise from Dr Johnson. I could see him fighting, grappling with his lungs. This was it.

Miles knew it too but he pulled on the alarm cord anyway. He ran out into the corridor, shouting for a nurse, doctor, Matthew, anyone. He ran back in. He ran back out and all the time Dr Johnson was struggling to get enough air to say ...

"Miles, stop," I said, following him out into the corridor. The alarm was buzzing away somewhere around the next corner. "Your father wants to tell you something."

"But where is everyone?" Miles shouted. I grabbed him and dragged him back into the room where poor old Dr Johnson was still trying to inflate his lungs to say ...

"Listen," I said. "It's over, Miles. Listen to your

father."

It was their last chance. I was breathing with Dr Johnson again: suck, gasp, wheeze, suck ... and then finally he was ready. He opened both his eyes and said, "The bitch." There was a long gurgling out-breath and ... nothing.

Now Miles was yelling and crying and banging on his father's chest. I pulled him away and he hit me. Great. But I stood between him and the bed and his ex-father and I wouldn't let him past and suddenly the room was full of nurses and doctors and God knows who else ... some Johnsons as well ... and I couldn't hold back that many people. It wasn't my business anyway. I just hoped he'd really gone. I hoped they wouldn't get him back.

And then somehow I was out in the corridor. So was Miles. My eye was swelling up and he was holding his hand like a wounded puppy paw.

"You bastard," he was yelling at me. "You total fucking bastard. I could've saved him."

I looked at him. He looked at me. His mouth was hanging open and foaming a weird pale beige froth. It reminded me, Christ knows why, of the foam on the top of the coffee they used to serve in those horrible Pyrex glass cups in the diner by the bus station in Limerick.

"No you couldn't," I said.

He tried to hit me again but I ducked out of the way and he put his fist through a seaside watercolour. They liked seaside watercolours at The Portesham.

"Ow," he said. His knuckles were dripping dark

red blood onto the carpet. It didn't show.

"I'm going now," I said. Enough. I went to look for some breakfast.

But there was nowhere to get the kind of breakfast I wanted, not in fucking Chelsea, and I couldn't face a cab ride or any more walking so I ended up sitting on a bench at a bus stop. Then I realised I was just round the corner from Angus's building so I went the final few yards and sat in the bijou little garden instead. I didn't care about the Welsh occupation. They didn't know who I was. I had no fight with them anyway. After a while Miles pitched up.

"I followed you," he said. "I'm sorry."

"That you followed me?"

"No," he said. He tried to give me a hug but it was clumsy, something like trying to put up a deck chair that's been left out all winter, and he wiped blood on my shirt.

"I'll never get that out," I said.

"No."

We sat there.

"I'm ready for a fag," I said. Someone had to say something.

"Me too."

This surprised me but actually I didn't care what Miles did to his lungs anymore.

"That was so awful," he said. "So totally fucking awful. They shouldn't have left him."

Who shouldn't? His fucked up family? Maybe they'd stayed up all night, waiting.

"I expect they were tired," I said. Like me. Of you.

"Tired? D'you know how much they charge?"

Not his family then.

"I expect they had an emergency," I said. The word sounded wrong, more like a birth than a death.

"So what was that then?" Miles was angry again. He needed someone to hate. Again. "What was that if it wasn't an emergency?"

"I expect they were trying to save someone who could actually be ... saved," I said.

"I can't believe they left him alone like that," Miles said.

"It wouldn't have made any difference, Miles. He wanted to die. He was having a crap time."

"It would've made a difference. We said we were going to be there for him."

So we were back on the family. I personally thought that Dr Johnson had been waiting for them all to go away so he could die in peace. Miles turning up at the critical moment had just been a final slap of bad timing.

"I can't believe I let him down like that," Miles was saying. "Did you hear what he said?"

"Er ..." He didn't wait for an answer. Luckily.

"I can't believe I spent the night locked in a larder with a pissed up child when I should've been at my father's bedside," he said.

Now that sounded wrong, the wrong words, too heavy on the melodrama. Aha. I could see where we were going with this.

"I can't believe I got so wrecked I forgot my dad was dying," he said next.

Yup. So what to do to stop the slide? He was going to pull me down with him, and the bench and the bijou garden and anything else that got in the way, down, down into a swirling vortex of miserable whining with Dr Johnson at the bottom in a Dracula outfit, laughing, laughing ...

I don't know why I couldn't just tell him to shut the fuck up. But I couldn't, so I said:

"Let's get a cab to the nearest bacon sandwich."

Too late. Miles' head was in his hands and he was leaking splashy tears onto the brick path arrangement.

"Oh God," he wept. "I'm the biggest bastard failure. I can't believe ... " etc. etc.

There were a lot of things he couldn't believe. After a while I felt I should stop him.

"Look," I said. "It's not all bad."

I placed a consoling hand on his back, pat, pat, while I struggled to think of something to say: cholera, perhaps. In the end you turn black and die. Apparently. Or it could be the other way round. I wasn't sure ... but anyway this technique always works for me. Whenever I'm feeling totally crap I think about how much more crap everything could be. Elephantitis is a strong favourite ... have you ever seen a picture?... Dafur, insurance broker. Surrey. Dr Johnson was well off out of it. But Miles wasn't going to be consoled.

"It's not all bad?" he yelled into my face. "How

could it get any worse?"

"Well ... actually, there's something you should know." I had to tell him sometime. There was something very wrong about his night in the larder, something almost incestuous, like he could end up being the ex-shag of the daughter of his ex-girlfriend's ex-shag, depending on how things worked out: a triple x-rating. No wonder it was all wrong. Anyway, I thought he needed to know and he was so down already he couldn't get much lower.

"Did you shag Electra?" I said.

"Oh my God," he groaned, head back in hands. "Don't tell me she's got herpes. Gonorrhoea? Syphillis?"

"So you did shag her?" I felt that my technique might be about to work its magic.

"Yes," he said.

"Then you should know that while you were humping away in the larder her father was getting it on with Sally."

"What? I don't fucking believe it."

Another thing he didn't believe but instead of seeing the up-side ... he hadn't caught the clap from an eighteen-year-old schoolgirl after all, how lucky was he ... he bent right over, like he was about to throw up between his feet, groaning like a sick cow. And then he lunged at me, a despairing kind of flinging move, and started to sob into my shirt collar. I could feel the wet soaking through to my neck. I was still trying to pat him better, there, there, when two men came out of Angus's building. One of

104

them said something as they walked past. It wasn't English. It was ... Welsh, of course, and although I don't speak Welsh I knew he was saying, "Look at that, Dai. More fucking poofters."

It was time to move on.

I thought that moving on might stop Miles going over and over and over how utterly crap he was, The Portesham had turned out to be, his family were, he was, dying was, shagging Electra had been, he was, he was, he was ...

I turned into a newsagent's in a suitably seedy street and bought the strongest packet of fags in the place, imports from Iraq. I gave one to Miles. We stood outside the shop door and lit up like a couple of shady rent boys. Miles turned green ... really green ... and threw up in the gutter. He dropped his cigarette and stamped it out, shaking his head in a rather irritating way.

"Why are you shaking your head?" I said. I was feeling somewhat soupy myself.

"I should've known," he said. I waited to see what it was he should've known but he didn't say anything else and I was too bored with him to be arsed. Actually, I was almost at that point where I was looking for a fight, maybe the fight to end all fights and then I'd never have to see him again. I walked on. He followed. After a while he started with the it's all crap stuff again, but like he was telling me for the first time.

Then I saw a cafe, a proper caff that looked like

they slaughtered the bacon out the back.

"D'you want some breakfast?" I said, just to shut him up.

"What? Oh, yes. Thanks."

Which implied I was buying. Ultimate fucking cheek. Right at that moment I would've preferred to blind myself with a white plastic fork than spend any more time in Miles' company ... but the fight had gone out of me. I'd been totally sapped by his non-fucking-stop monologue of everything being total, utter crap ... and, to be fair, the Snowdonian cocaine consumption and forty minutes sleep and oceans of booze and God knows what else. But it was him that was pushing me over the edge.

"Come on, then," I said. You cunt, I thought.

We sat at the back, away from the sun, and Miles was still going on and on and on ... I amused myself by peeling my arms off the tablecloth over and over and over. I liked the noise: skin leaving oilcloth, skin leaving oilcloth, skin leaving ... and Miles was still going on and on and on ...

"Miles," I said. "Your father's dead."

He was slightly stunned by my interruption.

"I know he is," he said. "But I can't believe ... "

"Yeah, I know," I said. "You already told me. The point is, do you want sausages and bacon or just bacon? Or black pudding?"

"You're supposed to be my friend," he said.

"I am," I lied. "That's why I'm saying stop now and order some breakfast."

"So you want me to shut the fuck up?" he said,

which was the first bit of incisive thinking I'd seen from him in some time. His voice was getting louder. People were turning round and staring. They thought we were having a domestic. "I can't believe you're telling me to shut up," he said, approaching full volume. His voice bounced around the cafe. Interesting, I thought. Formica has a natural reverb effect. "You've got no fucking idea, have you?" He was shouting now. "My dad's just died and you won't even let me talk about it. You don't know what it's like to see your father die right in front of you and there's nothing you can do about it. You don't know what ... "

"Yes I do," I said.

"No you don't," he yelled. My, the Johnsons were a bad tempered family. I wondered if they were any better without Death stalking them ... I doubted it, somehow. Anyway ...

"Yes I do," I said calmly. "I was there when my father died." It was a simple statement but it did shut him up. "I was there when my father died," I said again. I wasn't sure I'd ever said it before and now I'd said it twice. "I was there when my father died." Three times. Oh fuck.

We looked at each other across the sticky table.

"Were you?" Miles said. Quietly.

"Yeah. We were on our way back from the races, just me and him. He was pissed. I put my seat belt on because I could see he was fucking legless, actually. Some friends tried to stop him driving but the stupid fucker wouldn't listen. It was a Daimler, the powder blue one."

We had a lot of Daimlers.

"He was trying to light a fag and the cigar lighter wasn't working ... or it was but he was too slow with it and he kept on trying to put it back in the hole to have another go and he forgot to look at the road."

I could remember it so clearly, the cow parsley whipping against the windscreen, the hope that it would still be alright, still be alright if only my fucking father would get the fucking car under control ...

"We went up a bank and she flipped over and back onto the road and then we went along on the roof for ... "

Ages, it seemed. But it could still be alright. We were upside down and he was swearing and not that bothered about lighting his fag any more.

"We were doing fifty when he rolled it. I didn't know. That's what the police said after."

I remember him still trying to steer, even though we were on the roof and screaming towards a junction. But it could still be alright.

"We crashed into a horse box. They were waiting to pull out at this junction and we ran under the back of them. I got out through my window. My daddy was stuck. He was too big and he was mashed up anyway. Then the car caught fire."

The problem with electric fuel pumps, the police said after. The engine was still running so the fuel was still pumping.

"The people in the horse box wouldn't help me.

They were getting their horses out of the side ramp and they didn't give a fuck about my da. I don't blame them. The horses were fine. They took them away and then they came back to see if there was anything to be done but there wasn't. He was stuck. There was nothing to be done. He was banging on his window and shouting at me and I was just standing in the road, looking at him being burnt alive. I was ten."

"Fucking hell," Miles said. "What was he shouting?"

"Do something, you stupid little bastard."

"That was the last thing he ever said to you?"

"No. Well, yes. He also said Aaargh a lot, and Jesus save me and a lot of stuff like that but that was more general. He wasn't saying it to me."

"Fucking hell," Miles said.

I realised then that everyone in the cafe had been listening.

"So ... is it toast or fried bread with that?" I said.

12

After breakfast I stood outside the cafe. I was still hoping Miles would go away. I didn't want him around any more. I hadn't wanted him around in the first place but now the gig was done I wanted him around even less. And I really wanted to untell him about my father. He was going to use it to be my best friend. He was doing it now, that best mates thing, standing there with his hands in his pockets, watching me smoke.

I rang Angus.

"What?" he said.

"How's the house?"

"Alright."

"Clean?"

"Yeah. I can't talk now. I'm buying a goldfish bowl." He hung up.

This made things easier with Miles but I was still going to try to shake him off.

"So," I said. "What are you going to do next?"

He shrugged. He watched me put the filter to my mouth, breathe in, hold, breathe out.

"You need to see your family," I said.

"No. I don't."

"They'll be expecting you, Miles. You need to be together."

"No we don't. I realised something this morning. I don't like them."

"No-one likes their family," I said.

"Did you hear what Dad said?"

"Er ... " I said, trying to look like I was thinking hard.

"He said 'The bitch', didn't he? About Mum?" He was shaking his head again, looking down at a point just beyond the toes of his shoes, my shoes. I wondered if this was his new thing to do. I wondered if it was coming loose and how easy it would be to rip it off his neck. "And your dad said 'You useless little bastard'."

So this made us best mates now?

"He said stupid, not useless." He was still shaking his fucking head. "Is there something wrong with your neck?" I had to get away from him. I don't do sympathetic. Now there was no chance of a tour there was no chance whatsoever I could keep it up. Dr Johnson's status was immaterial. He'd had as much from me as he was going to get. "Look, I need to be on my own for a while," I said.

"Yeah," Miles said. "I'm going to see Jessica." WHAT? No no no no no ...

"That's the worst idea," I said. "In a weekend full of bad ideas, that's the worst."

"I've got to tell her about Electra."

"Don't do that."

"And Dad." He was biting his thumb again.

"Don't do that. You must not do that. Think about it, Miles. You're really fucked up at the moment.

Don't dump it on Jessica."

"I won't."

"You will. And you'll start smoking again. You won't be able to not. You promised, Miles. You promised your father. You can't go back on it now he's ... er ... deceased." I was careful about this but it sounded more like diseased anyway. "You need to come home with me and rest up for a while," I ploughed on. "Send her a text or something. She'll understand. Tell her you'll see her when you're more ... sorted. She'll really admire you for that."

Miles was looking at me like I was a lovely man but at least he'd stopped shaking his head.

"Do you want it to work between us?" he said.

No, you stupid wanker, of course I don't. But there was nothing Jessica loved more than somebody else's crisis. Here was the best reason to pack her bag and say goodbye to her fellow inmates. She'd be out by tea-time, coping, sharing, shagging, suggesting a bottle of Jack Daniels for the pain ... and there we'd go again. And the thing she loved second best was seeing off the competition. She'd mince Electra into 130lbs of pie filling with one look, one thrust of a bitch knife from hell comment. I couldn't have that, not now. I had no prospects. I had nowhere else to go. Fuck. Think of the carnage. Think of Jessica unleashed. Think of no money. No no no. I needed a plan. I needed a job. I needed an escape route, just in case ...

"Whatever," I said. "But I have to protect her. Come home now. We'll talk. I'll do some laundry.

I'll show you some pics of her on her pony."

That did it. Miles put his arm around my shoulders and gave me a best mates squeeze.

"You're my family now," he said.

And at that point I changed my mind.

All this ... all of it, everything that had happened was down to Dr Johnson extracting a pointless promise from his son. It wasn't random fate or fucked up coincidence or just plain unfortunate. It was the knock-on thing, the giving up of the fags on Friday night leading inevitably, inexorably to exactly, precisely where we were now, a farting bison in Minnesota starting a riot in Cairo. Or however it worked. As a parting shot it was as bad as it could get.

Angus was sitting at the kitchen table when we got back. The goldfish was in a bowl with a sunken galleon and a treasure chest to play with. He was arranging some weed for it.

"They need privacy," he said. "Something to hide in. If they want." I suddenly felt I had a lot in common with the goldfish. "That's what the girl in the shop said."

"So whose goldfish is it?" I said.

"Yours," he said, "unless you know where it came from. But you don't, do you?"

"No." I sat down opposite him. Miles sat down too.

"And while we're on the subject ... " What subject? Angus was pulling a notebook out of a back pocket, checking the figures, "you owe me £730."

"Does that include the cost of the goldfish bowl?"

"No."

"So can you give me a breakdown on that?"

"Sure," he said. He checked his notebook again. "Coca: £530. Sambuca run: near enough £90, with the taxi. Goodnight mix: £110."

"Goodnight mix?"

"The blue wraps. When you ran out of coke. I did tell you not to. It finished the party. No-one can stay awake on that. It's my own recipe." He smiled proudly.

"Right," I said. "Have you got any grass?"

"Yeah. How much d'you want?"

"How about we round it up to £800? I can't have you financing my fish. Make the rest up in sticky buds and I'll sort you out tomorrow."

We moved through to the sitting room. Angus had a pipe. We sat around, smoking little shots of his finest herb, now my herb. I put on some Charlie Parker. Miles seemed O.K. Angus was telling him about his mother in Tangier. If you didn't know any better you could've mistaken us for three chilled out chums enjoying a Sunday afternoon blitz ... but I could tell Miles was just in some kind of lull. Or it could be shock. I was sure there'd be more from him later. And Angus was high on the notion that he'd quit the coke simply by selling his personal to me. The Welsh had the rest, whatever was stashed

114

away in his flat, now their flat.

"It's all gone," he said. "So that's it."

Of course. It really was that simple. I wondered how long it would take for his delusions to turn to mania. If Miles weren't so weird right now we could sneak off into the kitchen and have a bet on it.

I went into the kitchen anyway, to check on the fish.

My housemates followed me. Miles was telling Angus about his father and how he was like some T.V. chef ... some fat woman on a motorbike. But he was O.K. and it seemed to make sense to Angus.

"Did you get any food?" I asked Angus.

"I already fed him," he said.

"I meant food for us."

"Food?" he said, like I'd asked for a bottle of carbonated Martian spring water. "I don't eat."

"Ever?" Miles said. "Not even a sandwich?"

I opened the larder door, although I knew there was nothing in there apart from a bag of pearl barley and a tin of artichoke hearts ... and some bloke. He looked up at me from the bed of shamefully crap shags. I shut the door again.

"Who the fuck's that?" I said.

"That's Angelo," Angus said. "I said he could stay in there."

"For how long?"

"Till he was well enough to walk home. He helped clear up."

Angelo looked ... Spanish or something.

"Where does he live?" I said.

"Don't know. He's from Bolivia."

"Look," I said. "I can't have any more people staying here. You're O.K, Miles is O.K, but Angelo's got to go."

I went back into the sitting room. Miles and Angus followed me. We smoked some more grass. Miles put on Cold Play. Angus talked over the top about his mother in Tangier. I sat in a corner of the amusingly chintzy Chesterfield and flicked through an old copy of Cosmopolitan. I was worrying about where I was going to find £800. As a kept man I just didn't have that kind of cash lying around. And there was no room for a spot of financial fiddling: my delightful sister had everything under remote control, everything on standing order or account or whatever it was she'd set up when she was making slightly more sense and a zillion quid every fifteen minutes. The band hadn't earnt any serious money in months. And when it did it got spent on fun, fun, fun. Fuck it, fuck it, fuck it. This was all Dr Johnson's fault.

But wait ... maybe I could ask Kate Moss for a loan. She must've been paid a good whack for the lippie ad. She'd understand. Even better ... maybe I could charge my housemates rent, in advance. Including Angelo that would be a mere £100 a week each, two weeks up front plus a week's notice. It sounded good in my head. Kate wasn't so sure.

I looked at them over the top of the mag.

With her as the foreground they looked much,

much worse and worse than that, I was suddenly suspicious that somehow, through sloth or robbery or bad investments or something they were broke, the bastards. There was still Angelo though, who was showing no signs of setting off on his long trek back to Bolivia. But £300 a week from one tenant did seem a bit steep, even for this fabulous palace of shit. Kate was shaking her head like I was a poor crazy mixed up kid ... or could it be the DTs finally catching up with me.

Enough. I turned the page. The doorbell rang.

"Who's that?" Angus said.

I went to see.

Electra was standing on the doorstep.

"I've come round to get my stuff," she said.

I didn't know she had any stuff. I personally thought she'd come round to see if there was any point in a second attempt with Miles or any chance of getting it back on with me. It was Sunday afternoon. She was bored.

"Why did you ring the bell?" I said.

"I can't just walk in," she said, meaning everything there was to say about the change in her status, how sensitive she was being to this, what a bastard I was etc. etc.

"But it doesn't work," I said. She extended a forefinger to press the bell. She bit her nails. I'd never noticed that before. She made contact. The bell rang.

"Yes it does," she said.

"I mean it didn't. I pulled the wires out, remember?"

She looked at me critically, trying to work out if this was an attempt to win her back with a we-did-have-fun-sometimes reminder. It wasn't, which she saw right away. She also saw that I was very stoned and therefore talking crap.

"You fucking useless shit," she said. She pushed past me and flounced off down the hall to pick up her hair grip. I watched her go. There was nothing hey-Tom Bombadillio about her purple ballet pumps today. Then I remembered about her mother. And then about her father and Sally.

I went back into the sitting room and sat back down on the Chesterfield, feeling like I should be feeling like I was a mean and nasty man. I tried for a while to get there ... no. Failed again. I was too stoned to care. Anyway, she shagged my best friend. I owed her nothing.

The doorbell rang.

"Who's that?" Angus said.

I went to see.

I opened the front door. The porch was packed with big square-shaped men, mining type men in black leather jackets like Vinny Jones in a gangster movie.

I tried to close the front door but one of them stuck a foot in it. Fuck. We were dead.

And then I realised, with my sloth brain working at the speed of spilt treacle, that it couldn't be the

Welsh. They'd be inside by now and doing whatever it was they'd come round to do. They wouldn't be waiting for an invitation.

I tried to close the door again anyway. The foot stayed. It was wearing a big black boot.

I gave up with the door closing and opened it instead. It was the only thing to do, apart from run, and that wouldn't work for more than .3 of a second.

"Good afternoon, gentlemen," I said. They were all over the steps as well, and down the path. "Have you come to claim your fish?"

There was a ripple effect at shoulder level, something like gears turning in liquid tarmac, and Luke appeared at the front of the mob. He was blue and purple in places, and stitched.

"Alright, Luke?" I said.

"No he's fucking not." The voice came from the back, somewhere by the gate. The front row just carried on standing there, looking down at me. It was a good trick. I felt my bowels drop. "Show him, Lucas."

Luke smiled. His front teeth were missing.

"These are my brothers," he said. "And some of my cousins. They want to talk to your mate Angus."

"I wouldn't exactly call him my mate," I said. I felt it was important to clear this up. "You'd better come in."

The thing' was, Luke was a Sharpe. Angus understood what this meant. The Sharpe family didn't have a problem with Angus. His business was his business. They didn't have a problem with that. Spike Sharpe, the voice of the Sharpes, sat on the amusingly chintzy Chesterfield and told us this more times than he needed to. We ... me, Miles, Angus ... understood what he meant. The man had a rare gift for understated menace.

The thing was, they'd all worked really hard when they were kids to buy a trumpet for Luke and pay for music lessons and then put him through music school.

"Mum couldn't do it on her own," Spike said. "We all pulled together. That's what we do."

We understood what he meant.

Angelo came in then. He wanted to know if anyone wanted a cup of tea. Various Sharpes said things like Cheers, mate or Have you got any coffee? and we ... me, Miles, Angus ... started to breath again, but very politely .

The thing was, the Sharpes wanted to kill the men who'd knocked out Luke's front teeth and ruined his career. They'd found his trumpet. That was all Spike said: "We found his trumpet."

We understood what he meant.

They wanted Angus's address. They knew about the Welsh but they didn't know where they were. They were going to pay them a visit, give them a little private education. They were going to get his flat back. Then they were going to kick the fuckers out of London. Right out.

"I don't want my flat back," Angus said.

120

"You're getting it back," Spike said.

"Great. Thanks," Angus said. "But they've got my suppliers. I can't do sweet fuck all without my suppliers."

"You're getting your flat back," Spike said.

"Thanks," Angus said. "Great."

I was wondering if the Sharpes had heard of the amazing advances in dentistry in the 21st century: bridges, crowns, whole new gobs of teeth. I was wondering if I should tell them before gang warfare broke out and the streets were running with blood and more people got arrested or were forced to dress up in frocks and go out in public or needed stitches or somewhere to stay for a while or an undertaker.

But maybe that wasn't the point.

Even if Luke could have his teeth completely restored maybe that wasn't the point.

Angelo came in with a tray. I was getting to like him. And then I thought maybe, just maybe in all this mess and potential blood and bone and mayhem there was a way here to write off the £800 … or at least buy some time. I was just warming up with this one when Electra came into the sitting room. She stood just inside the door. There wasn't anywhere much else for her to stand.

"I just want to say," she said, "that I think you are a total shit." She'd been crying upstairs all this time, I realised, expecting me to go to her or whatever it was that decent blokes did. I'd actually forgotten she was there. I was entertaining the Sharpes. That took my full attention.

"What's on here?" Spike said.

"You said we were going to be friends," Electra said across the roomful of Vinny Jones look-alikes. She didn't seem to have noticed they were there. But whatever, this was clearly rubbish.

"I'd never say anything as cheesy as that," I said. "That's almost as bad as it's not me, it's you."

"Don't you mean it's not you, it's me?" Spike said.

"Oh. Yeah. Of course," I said. "But I didn't say it."

"You did," she said. "You said I could always talk to you about … stuff."

"You did," Angus said. "You said she could always rely on you. To be her friend. You did."

Fuck off, Brutus, I thought, but I didn't say that either. I just stood there while everyone looked at me like I was a mean, nasty man. Again. This is typical of blokes. Just when you think you'll get some bloke solidarity they all turn against you. Luckily at this point Electra decided to leave.

"Is that your girlfriend?" Spike asked me when the front door had slammed behind her.

"Was. She was my girlfriend."

"Isn't she a bit … young?"

"Yeah. That's why I finished it. She's going out with him now."

I pointed at Miles. Or rather, I pointed at where Miles had been sitting. He wasn't there.

13

The thing was, the Sharpes were leaving. And as a special Sunday treat, we were going too. They told us this with that special Sharpe smile.

I wondered briefly if there was any way out, other than death ... but of course there wasn't. We had to go because it was kind of our fault that little Lukey was now minus his front teeth. We needed to realise how careless we'd been. We needed to understand what happened if you messed with the Sharpes. This was what they did: retribution, payback, breaking heads ... all in a day's work, mate. It was all about family honour. They were prepared to let it go this time but in the future they wanted us to take much, much better care of little bro Lucas.

But actually, we had to go anyway. They knew that we knew this. We had to stick with them because if battle was joined, and it would be, and the Welsh then somehow cut round the back of the Sharpe army, which they would do, and found us ... me, Miles, Angus and now Angelo ... wrecked in Clapham we really would be dead, not just scared to death but actually dead.

They'd think we'd sent them.

They'd think we'd mobilised the Sharpes ... for

the gig, for Angus, for the take-over of his place, his business, his patch, for the invasion of Louis' Place, Sharpe territory, for the ruination of Lucas Sharpe's career.

That's what I'd think. There were enough reasons to want to get even.

They were re-grouping in the hall and out in the porch. Angus got my point straight away. He agreed it would be suicide to stay in the house, even if we were allowed. He agreed that the Welsh would have no trouble tracking us down: they'd found him in Louis', they'd find us hiding in the airing cupboard. He also agreed that this thing had totally got away from us.

"We're fucking pissy little pawns," he said, "in the great game of life. But I still don't want my flat back." He whispered this in my ear when he thought the Sharpes weren't listening. "I mean, how are they going to stop them, the brothers and cousins and next door fucking neighbours in fucking Pontypridd? They should know that. They're all bloody related … them." He nodded towards the clan in the hall when he thought they weren't looking. "It's one fucking family against the massed fucking forces of the men of fucking Harlech. How many pissed off ex-miners do they think there are looking for a new career? I'll tell you. Fucking millions, mate."

This was the old Angus back again. I gave him the pipe and a pat on the back.

Meanwhile, it seemed that Angelo was up for anything and Miles was good for nothing. He was having another crisis. He'd tucked himself down between his chair and the sitting room wall and was refusing to move, speak, anything.

"Look, Miles," I said. "Things might be bad but if you don't come out they could get a whole lot worse."

"We have to go with them," Angelo said. "You're English, yeah? You like blood sports."

"We can't stay here," I said. "We want revenge just as much as they do, don't we? For Luke and his teeth and Angus and the gig. And your brother, Miles. Don't forget your brother."

"D'you think we're happy?" Angus said. "We're fucking not, mate. So stop dicking around like you're the prize fucking casualty and get ready for battle."

Miles curled up tighter.

"Let me deal with this," I said to Angus. "Look, Miles. You might be feeling crap right now but Luke and his brothers are about to go and stir up so much shit it'll be like … like the Hoover dam bursting, only with raw sewage."

"And bits of fucking pink bog roll and used Tampax and … "

"Angus? Let me deal with this. Look, Miles. None of us want to end up in deep shite but sometimes it just happens. And when it does you've just got to go with it … sink or swim."

"In a river of liquid shit," Angus said. "Closing over your head, mate."

"Angus? Shut the fuck up. Let's move the chair."

We pulled the chair away from the wall and dragged Miles to his feet. "Have a fag," I said. "For fuck's sake, have a fag." I tried to push a cig into his mouth. His jaw was clamped shut.

"What's the matter with one little cigarette?" Angelo said. "You feel better, it's good."

"Listen to the expert," Angus said. "You're not going to get lung cancer in one more fucking day, are you? It's all about crisis management."

"He's worried about lung cancer?" Angelo said. "In my country we don't worry about lung cancer. We don't live long enough. Listen, Miles. In my country little children smoke all the time. Their parents don't worry. They die of something soon enough … nothing to eat, sometimes floods, mud slides, hit by a truck. Or disease … a little malaria, blood poison, a touch of cholera and poomf: gone. There are a lot of ways to die."

"Yes, thank you, Angelo," I said. Miles was getting more rigid with every example of death not by smoking. I could hear leaving noises from the hall. "Look, Miles. I prescribe a cigarette to relieve your symptoms. We need you back on line, mate. You're a total liability like this. Get hold of him, Angus. Get his gob open, Angelo." Miles was resisting. He was surprisingly strong … the strength of a madman, perhaps. "Here we go," I said cheerily, and popped the fag in. Angelo closed his mouth. I held his nose shut, so he couldn't sneakily breathe through it. Angus had him in an upright headlock. But it seemed to be working. He seemed to be relaxing … or dying. "Ease up on his windpipe," I said to Angus. "He can't get the smoke down."

I was quite enjoying myself. I think we all were, apart from Miles. It was like being back at school. Luke came in to see what was up.

"You ready?" he said. "What are you doing to Miles?"

"We're turning him into a man," Angus said.

"Or a corpse," Luke said and he shrugged, a comme ci, comme ça kind of shrug. As it turned out, he should know … man, corpse, all in a day's work, mate. We let go. Miles spat out the cigarette. Angelo caught it before it could make contact with the authentically knackered yet surprisingly expensive Turkish carpet. He was a useful guy to have around.

"I'm sorry about … you know," Luke said.

You know what? Getting us into a spot of savage gang warfare with the risk of death or even worse, an extended stay in a nick for the criminally insane?

"You know … coming round for tea without being asked," he said. "Mum would kill us if she found out."

Fine. Now that we had our etiquette problems sorted we could get on with some fun carnage.

"Is there any way at all you could not do this?" I said.

"I already said I was sorry," he said. Now he was hurt. What more could he say?

"No, not the tea thing," I said, and then I gave up. Nothing mattered any more. I was living in a film script.

"You bloody English," Angelo said. "In my country we drop round for tea all the time."

We went to battle in a convoy of black cabs. Luke rode with us. No-one spoke. I amused myself by trying to imagine how much worse things could get … but I couldn't. Even a visit to my mother would've been better than this. And as the shots of sticky buds started to wear off and surreal turned to real I began to suspect there could be a problem … other than the ones already listed. It occurred to me that it was possible we weren't just on a sightseeing tour.

Why would the Sharpes risk the extra baggage?

They wouldn't. I wouldn't.

So maybe we weren't just along to be shown how close we'd come to liquidation. Maybe we had a function in this. Maybe we were going to learn by experience. Which made everything worse again, although quarter of a mile back I'd thought that was impossible.

"How long does it take to get from mine to yours?" Angus said. He was opening the cab window, releasing the farts of fear. "I really need a shit."

"I don't think the current occupiers of your flat are going to be too keen on that," I said. Was he totally insane? "You can't go knocking on the fucking door and ask to use the bathroom."

"I meant after."

"Oh. After. So. Luke. How long does your average

pitched battle take these days? It's just that Angus needs a dump."

"You'd better go before," Luke said. "Never get into a fight when you need a crap. It looks bad if you take a beating and you … you know. As well."

Great. The tricks of the trade. I was learning so much.

We stopped around the corner from Angus's building. Ex-building. He was still telling me he didn't want his flat back, not on any terms, any chance he got.

"Not even if they all waste each other and it turns out that Wales sunk into the bastard Irish Sea last night," he said. "And the Severn Bridge is a pile of scrap metal in the Bristol Channel."

You could tell he was somehow hoping this might be the case, although he'd only just thought of it.

"Sunk," Angelo said. "You English and your bloody language. Sunk, sunk … " And he wandered off into the crowd of black leather jackets massing on the pavement, shaking his head. Miles followed him. He was shaking his head too, but without that Latin rythym. He looked more like he was being tailed by a swarm of bluebottles … if bluebottles swarm. And this was what I found myself thinking about: swarms or not of bluebottles. Now I was becoming concerned that it was me who was losing my mind, fretting over collective nouns as a pre-engagement warm-up technique … but why worry? We'd all be dead soon so our finer tuning was hardly an issue.

And now everyone was here. There was a move towards Spike … gather round, men … and we … me, Miles, Angus, Angelo … were called up to receive our orders: we had to knock on the door, which was alright, but then not run away, which wasn't. We had to look like we were a serious attempt at a truce, maybe even a deal, and while the Welsh were doubled up laughing at us but before they recovered enough to beat the crap out of us the Sharpe army would step out from behind the bushes in the bijou little garden and beat the crap out of them.

I wondered at the sophistication of this plan. It seemed Angus was having trouble with it too.

"But … er … won't that mean that we're … er … kind of in between you and them?" he said to Spike, which was brave of him.

"Yeah," Spike said.

"Right," Angus said. "I didn't realise you wanted us to … er … "

"You didn't realise?" Spike said. "He didn't realise." This said to his waiting army. "Tell me, my son … " and he paused for the sniggering to hush down, " … if you had of realised, what d'you think you'd be doing? Right now?"

Angus couldn't answer that one. I think at this point he was wishing he'd chosen a more law-abiding route through life. Still, looking on the bright side, he'd been lucky so far. And he might be lucky again in the future. It was just this weekend that was proving to be something of a problem.

"Well?" Spike said.

Angus still couldn't answer. The Sharpes made a black leather departure corridor through their ranks. It was time to go.

"Did you realise?" Angus said to me. We were getting close, trying to walk like a serious attempt at something. "Are they watching us?"

"They're all watching us," I said. "Every fucking one of them. What did you do all fucking day when it was your flat?"

"I didn't realise," Angelo said. "Do any of you guys know how to fight?"

"I didn't realise," Angus said. "Did you realise, Miles?"

Miles didn't answer. He was still being tailed by bluebottles.

"Miles didn't realise," Angelo said. "I'm worried about him."

"Why are you worried about Miles?" I said. "It's his fucking fault we're in this fucking mess in the fucking first place. Kind of." I was starting to sound like Angus. It was the stress. I seriously didn't want to end up like him … which was one more thing to get seriously stressed about. Shit.

"He didn't realise," Angelo said. He was a compassionate man.

Now we were walking up the path through the bijou garden. It seemed all wrong, the wrong place for breaking bones. Angus rang the bell for his flat

… ex-flat. His hand was shaking.

"I think I'm about to crap myself," he said.

"Yeah," I said. "Me too." I felt it brought us closer. But I didn't want to be closer …

"My dad died this morning," Miles said. "Doesn't that count for anything?"

"I think they're out," I said. "And no, not right now, Miles."

"They're not out," Spike said from somewhere, to our left. How did he know?

Angus rang the bell again. This was torture. I tightened my bum, just in case.

"They're not answering," Angus said. "Shall I use my key?"

"You've got a key?" I could hear the hidden Sharpes groaning: he's got a key … the fucking twat's got a key etc. "Why didn't you say?" I said.

"Of course I've got a fucking key," Angus said. "I live here."

"Then use it, you fucking mother fucker," Spike said. He was behind a viburnum. I could just make him out through the veil of delicate white flowers, Vinny in a lace mantilla. It was all wrong. Actually, on reflection, he was more like a psychotic Frank Lampard … but it was still all wrong.

Angus was trying to get the key into the lock but his hand was shaking.

"Give it to me," I said. "Let's get this over with."

We … me, Miles, Angus, Angelo … were in the hall now, walking across the classy black and white tiles to the stairs, walking along the corridor towards Angus's front door, knocking on the door …

"Why aren't they answering?" Angus said. "Are they going to pull some fucking stunt or what?"

"Maybe they went out after all," Angelo said. "It's the most likely explanation."

"We should be ready anyway," I said.

I could hear a bell ringing hard in the flat.

And banging from downstairs.

I made two pathetic fists, trying to look like a serious attempt at something before I died … ouch. I looked down at my right hand. The key to the front door was still in it. Oh my fucking Lord.

"They can't get in," I said. "The Sharpes can't get in."

I tried to give Angus his key back. He didn't want it.

"Fucking hell," he said. "Why didn't you leave it in the door? You've locked them out. What are we going to do now?"

"But they were already out," I said, like it was going to make any difference. "Oh fuck."

The Sharpes would never believe this was a genuine mistake … ever. Everyone looked at me like I was the biggest twat on earth. Even Miles was managing to sneer.

"We're in trouble now," Angelo said. "For sure."

This was fucking ridiculous. Suddenly I was bored with it. And then, even though we had no back-up, not even back-up that wanted to see us in traction, I decided to give Angus's ex-front door a good kicking … just to see what would happen next, because something had to happen. The suspense was killing me. It wasn't one of my better ideas but nothing happened anyway.

"I've got a key," Angus said. "If you want."

I wondered, not for the first time, how bright Angus actually was … but possibly I needed to concentrate on the job in hand. So where the fuck were they? Trying to fix their Bren gun? Loading their machine pistols? Breaking up Angus's furniture into vicious but very expensive clubs? So many questions whirring round and round in my head … so many possibilities … so many ways to die … so why were we still standing here?

"Is there another way out?" I said.

"There's a fire escape down the back," Angus said.

"So let's fucking go."

"Are you crazy?" Angus said. "We can't run away."

"Why not? We're fucked whatever we do. We might get away with it. It's worth a try."

This suddenly seemed to make sense to my comrades, more sense anyway than standing outside a front door waiting to get shot or whatever.

"I suppose calling the police is completely out of the question?" Miles said.

"I'd say definitely on that one," I said.

"That's a shame," he said. "What a shame."

"But not as much of a shame as Angus going down for twenty years for dealing cocaine," I said.

"Excuse me, officer, but a bunch of nasty thugs have just muscled in on my highly lucrative but totally illegal little business. Could you tell them to go away, please? Jesus, Miles. How unbelievably dumb are you? So ... what's it to be, boys?"

United at last, we turned as one man and ran for the back of the building, pushing on the fire door, all of us together, a bolting beast of eight arms, eight legs ... out onto the fire escape, down the metal stairs, back at ground level in another bijou garden with high brick walls and an attractive razor wire deterrent ...

"How the fuck do we get out of here?" I said.

"Round the front," Angus said.

"But that's no fucking good."

"Er ... no. Fuck."

"Stop, stop a minute," Angelo said. "Listen."

We listened. He was right. I could hear the sweet sound of sirens approaching ... shouting, smashing, thwacking, and feet on the gravel running towards us round the side of the building ...

"Back, back," I shouted, because suddenly everything was clear. We ran back up the fire escape two, three steps at a time ... back into the building, pulling the door slam shut just as two bloody faces got to it ... too late. We kept on running, along the corridor away from whoever it was ... my money was on the Welsh ... that was now trying to break down the fire door so they could break our legs or shoot us or whatever.

"I don't get it." Angus looked like he was about

to expire. His face had a touch of the morgue about it and he was struggling for air. "What the fuck's going on?"

"They went down the fire escape," I said. "They saw us coming. They went down the fire escape and round the front and jumped the Sharpes."

So in the end it was just boys' stuff, a game of tag played by psychopaths … but I would ponder this later. If I was still alive, of course.

"We've got to go and help Luke," I said.

"Are you totally fucking insane?" Angus wheezed at me. He sounded like Dr Johnson … not what he was saying, of course, but how he was saying it.

"You should give up smoking," I said.

"He's right," Angelo said.

"Who's right?" I said. We were at the top of the stairs now. The sirens were getting closer.

"You are," Angelo said. "If we don't, he's dead."

"Who's dead?" I said.

"You are, my friend."

"But just now you were all for running away," Angus gasped.

That was when I thought I could, sloth brain. Keep up.

"You have to learn to go with it, Angus," I said. "Things change."

They certainly did.

14

Two hours later, Miles was a hero and I was technically homeless. I was allowed to stay in the summer house at the end of the garden until I'd found somewhere to live. That was my best offer. Meanwhile, Jessica was chopping lines of the purest uncut amphetamine sulphate on the kitchen table for Spike 'Coke is for Wimps' Sharpe but not doing any herself and Angus was in a taxi, heading for Heathrow. Angelo had been sent to find Jack Daniels and beer and maybe some food for everyone who hadn't gone home to their cheerful Cockney wives and rosy-cheeked children … he came to tell me he was just popping out, in case I was worried … and the best part? I now owed Spike £800 for a molehill of inconsequential party dust, the use of which marked me down forever as a pathetic poofter.

And I was flat broke. Unless Jessica went back into rehab. So I was flat broke.

This was how things had changed.

So … three hours prior to this unfortunate turn of events we were standing at the top of the stairs in Angus's building. I'd perceived, if you recall, that the only way forward was to join the fight. We moved down the stairs to the front door, painted a fetching petrol blue. I'd never noticed this before.

We could hear the fighting. Angus's farts of fear had become unbearable. I had my hand on the latch. Angelo was right beside me, Angus and Miles were hanging back, shouting at me to stop, to wait: don't open the door. They didn't get the strategy. They didn't understand what Spike and co. would do to us if they thought there was any chance at all … no matter how small … that we'd somehow set this up with the Welsh. They didn't understand that they had to fight. They didn't want to.

Anyway, I opened the door because I had to.

It was clear immediately that things were not going well for the Sharpes. They were fighting hard but the Welsh must have called in reinforcements from somewhere … you couldn't fit that many people into Angus's flat … and they were seriously outnumbered. Still, it was also clear that everyone was having a great time, which was an angle I hadn't thought of: the Sharpes lived to scrap. It was about revenge too, of course, little Lukey's teeth and family honour and all that but they loved their work … which explained their pitiful battle plan. They weren't resigned to GBH as a last resort in a tight spot. It was their chosen profession.

It took me less than a couple of seconds to take this in, to pick an opponent who'd already taken an honest hammering, to turn the key in my fist for maximum damage … when Miles stepped up beside me. I knew straight away he was back from wherever he'd been. Real fear does that to you.

Anyway, he looked over the scene in the now totally trashed bijou little garden like he was some sort of demi-god stunt man action movie critic and said:

"It's all so utterly pointless."

That's what he said. And then he jumped into the fight ... actually, leapt is a better description, like a man jumping out of a plane, but without a parachute. And then I don't know what happened because Angus did a one-man Braveheart-style charge from way back in the hall and knocked me down the steps outside the front door which knocked me out cold so I missed it but Miles won the fight for the Sharpes. He was like a demon, Angelo said after, like a man possessed by the devil, a secret weapon.

The Welsh were totally thrown.

They didn't know how to deal with it.

It was almost cheating, unsporting, against the code of gangster combat, like to take him out would jinx you or hex you or something and while they were thinking about it the Sharpes grabbed the advantage. Maybe Chelsea had always been a bit of a long shot, a bit of a trek from the Valleys, like Napolean and Moscow. Whatever, they knew they were beaten, if not now then sometime in the future and all the fight went out of them. This is what Angelo said.

So Miles was the Sharpes' new mascot. They loved him and I regained consciousness too late to stop him texting Jessica on Angus's mobile. When I asked Angus what the fuck he thought he was doing he said he didn't care any more about my twisted little games, like the whole thing with Jessica, the whole fucking mess of it had been my idea ... which is the most screwed up, twisted fucking thing he's ever said ... and all he wanted was his passport and the £800 I owed him and he was gone, to Tangier to see his mother. Forever. You could call it running away, throwing in the towel, a pathetic chicken retreat ... whatever ... but actually it felt more like a horse bolting. He didn't care what was in front of him, as long as he got as far away as possible from what was behind him. Forever. It was all too much. Spike got involved at this point and ended up taking Angus's flat off him for my £800, which I now owed to him. When I tried to say that meant he'd just acquired a two bedroom flat in Chelsea for double fuck all, for absolutely no outlay whatsoever, Angus told me to keep out of Spike's business and what difference did it make who I owed the money to, which was so fucking stupid of him I couldn't think what to say back so I just stood there looking like a complete arse with my trousers round my ankles, trying to think of a way to make it work out better for me because earlier I'd thought ... I couldn't remember what I'd thought but I must have been concussed because right at that moment I couldn't think of anything Spike hadn't already thought of and then suddenly everyone hated me ... apart from Angelo, but he felt it shift. He told me later.

Anyway, it gets worse.

I thought everyone would go away next and leave me, Miles and Angelo to get a cab back to Clapham where I could at least put Miles straight on what was what but no … they all came back, making a big fuss of him like he'd saved Planet Earth from Total Destruction and was also related to Lassie. Angelo made tea and we all sat round the kitchen table and the talk went on and on and then various Sharpes started drifting off home until there were just seven or eight of them, including Spike and Luke, and us. Except by now us meant me and Angelo because Angus was already heading for the nearest airport and Miles had become an honorary Sharpe. Anyway, they were laughing about the 'crash' on the Hammersmith flyover … they actually did the inverted comma finger thing. How fucking sad is that? … and what a great idea it had been and how the sirens had whooped right on past the hottest bit of action in town ha ha ha when Jessica turned up.

I knew she would. I knew she'd come to find Miles, to skewer him and roast him over a slow fire, to baste his writhing body with her very own special recipe acid and ground glass barbecue sauce, slicing bits off when she felt like a bit of slicing and then spitting out his tortured bones when she was done … but then she saw Spike and everything changed.

She covered it well.

You couldn't tell, unless you were me.

She said she'd come home for the night to make sure everything was alright, that Miles and her big bro weren't in any kind of trouble, it was just that the text said there'd been a fight etcetera.

The Sharpes were staring at her. A couple of them

even stood up. She does good room entry, if you like upright serpents in Gucci and full make-up. It's her Actually, I am really together look, I'm just having a few problems right now look, but problems that make me fascinatingly complex and also a fantastic fucked-up lay. Luke wasn't staring, of course. Luke knew. He said he was going. I tried to get him to stay. My popularity rating was already dangerously low and without Luke on my side I was fucked. Jessica had the rest of the Sharpes and Miles and possibly Angelo. I needed Luke but he went anyway and we started the story of the fight again, so Jessica could hear all about it.

This was where Miles really missed his chance. And also where Spike made his move on Jessica because there was this Isn't he a clever little puppy dog? sub-plot to the way he told her the story. It was well buried but I could tell what he was up to. Miles could've turned it around. Jessica was looking at him sideways while she listened, and then back to Spike … Miles, Spike, Miles, Spike, Miles … but he was sitting all wrong to pull off surprisingly cool dude.

I could see her weighing it up: disjointed idiot or scaly psycho?

So really Spike was always going to win. Or lose, because Jessica is the worst booby prize in all of history, but he was a nasty nutter so what did I care? Miles had sort of realised what was going on by now but he still looked like Spike was patting him on the head with every word, which just made the puppy slur stick even better, digging his own little puppy dog grave. In the end it was never going to happen with Jessica, praise be, but he looked so pathetic I almost felt sorry for him.

Anyway, I let this run on until I saw Jessica looking at me. We'd got to the part where I was lying face down on the steps with my face in a flowerbed. Spike was saying I'd done a great job of faking being knocked out but at least my mates had some backbone. I was prepared to let this go, mainly because he was trying to wind me up to argue the point and it really is totally fucking pointless trying to argue with a psychopath. Anyway, I saw Jessica looking at me and I said, "What?" Which was stupid, I know, because now Spike had something to get hold of.

"What d'you mean, what?" he said.

"I mean what," I said.

Now everyone was looking at me. Jessica was delighted. She knew once I'd bitten I wouldn't let go. She also knew that having me around would mess up her Spike fun. She wanted me gone. They carried on looking at me, waiting for me to explain my what.

"Why d'you think it's so cute?" I said. Their hostility was making me itch.

"That's a why," Spike said. Everyone tittered.

"Alright," I said. "What's so cute about Miles punching a bunch of Welsh gangsters? His girlfriend threw him out, his dad died this morning and he's trying to give up the fags." I shrugged, like this combination would send the best of us a little schizo.

"So what does it take to get you to fight?" Spike said. I knew he really wanted to say 'fight like a man' but it was too naf, even for a psychopath. The temperature in the kitchen had dropped to zero.

"I don't have a girlfriend right now and my father's already dead," I said, "and I've got no plans to give up smoking but you can top my mother if you like. Then we'll see if it works for me."

Jessica did a horrified little gasp, like this was the most wicked thing I could've said, which was so outrageous it was actually quite funny because she'd spent her teenage years trying to convince me that we should murder the old bitch … but no-one else in the room would know that. Or believe me if I tried to explain. But I should've tried, I now realise, because I started to laugh at her, and at the remaining outraged Sharpes, for buying into such a stale mobster cliché … D'you hear that? D'you hear what he said? We might o' been bad boys but we always loved our muvver, we did … so there was absolutely zero chance they were going to get the joke and then, because by now everybody already thought I was a worthless piece of shit so basically I had nothing left to lose, I said to Spike:

"Could you stop doing that, please?"

He was using the goldfish bowl as an ashtray. Little fishy was swimming up to the surface and nibbling on the ash, which possibly wasn't going to kill him but it seemed so … callous, I suppose.

144

Unnecessary. And this from someone who's seen foxes getting ripped in half three times a week. It was the way he was doing it. There was an ashtray right by his elbow.

"This?" he said, and tapped a load more in.

Suddenly, I was the defender of the fish. It was the most important thing ever, to look out for the fish. It's the not letting go thing. That was it: the focus of it all, of everything, was the fish.

So Jessica, always happy to cause total carnage and hopefully worse, picked up a pinch of sulphate and sprinkled it onto the water, exactly like it was fish food. Fishy swum up to have a look, liked what he saw and got stuck in … nibble, nibble … while everyone laughed. Apart from me. And Angelo, who was wiping the draining board so he didn't have to watch. Oh, and Miles, who by now looked like a puppet with its strings cut.

What to do?

I stood up. Spike stood up. We stood there.

"Oh look," Jessica said. "We could enter your fish in the fishy Olympics."

My fishy friend was already doing accelerated laps of his bowl, a little orange blur of confusion, faster and faster …

Everyone laughed. Again. This was their idea of sport. But not Jessica's. She knew I knew what she was doing. And why. She really wanted me gone. Anyway, the next most interesting thing for this bunch of total morons, after a spot of fish torture, was to see how I was going to save my little friend.

He was bumping into his sunken galleon that Angus had bought for him, again and again. Jessica bent down to watch, looking through the side of the bowl and from where I was I could see her eyes, distorted by the curve of the glass and the water all mixed up by the fishy frenzy and I thought: you total, utter, utter bitch.

So I said it.

And she smiled, slowly, all pretty poison pixie and slowly, extra deliberately sprinkled on some more sulphate, in the way that you would idly poke someone with your dainty princess foot when you know you've already killed them and I hated her so much I kind of lunged across the table to get to her and Spike, predictably enough, suddenly turned into her defender and then boyfriend and grabbed me by the hair like I was a naughty schoolboy and somehow the goldfish bowl got knocked over and I was dragged outside through the French windows while everyone cheered, or possibly jeered, but I could see Angelo frantically trying to save the fish while the Sharpes were distracted, watching me getting slapped around. My, what a sporting evening it was turning out to be.

So ... this was how I was banished / chose voluntary exile, whatever, before Spike was forced to injure me in a permanent way. They all went back inside and carried on being total morons.

I went down the garden and sat in the dark for hours ... alright, an hour, but it seemed much longer, grieving for my fish, hating my sister for all eternity, thinking all this through …

… and what I mainly thought was: bollocks.

But I liked the summer house. I'd stayed here before. And looking on the bright side, it was summer. It didn't work so well in December but it was June this month so after a while I took a chair out onto the verandah and sat with my feet up on the breathtakingly expensive handcrafted balustrade and watched Jessica and her fan club through the French windows into the kitchen.

I started making a list in my head of things I had to do:

1. Pay back the £800
2.

Actually, 2 probably didn't matter. And although you might be thinking £800 isn't that much, surely he could scrape it together somehow, I knew I couldn't. I knew I was all out of options and anyway, £5 is a lot of money if you haven't got it. Spike had already told me what he thought of cocaine users. He'd already made it totally clear that he expected payment in full by Friday. There would be no reprieve. I wondered if his attitude would be more flexible if it was a debt for a dinky sidearm or a Cost Cutter's carrier bag packed with Semtex. Probably.

Angelo came out of the French doors and on down the garden. He was carrying a tray: my dinner and a six pack of beers.

"It's not so good in there," he said. He sat down on the verandah steps. "Your sister's one fucked up lady. But I think the fish is O.K. I think he'll pull through. He's a tough little cookie."

Praise the Lord. Something good in all this utter crap.

"Thanks, Angelo," I said. "You don't have to stay, you know. You could go home." And I could go with you … to Bolivia, perhaps. Mmmm … tinned artichokes mashed into soup. My favourite. "Is this what everyone else had?" I said.

"No," he said. "I can't go. I can't leave Miles."

"What's up with him now? He was doing alright before. So what did you have?"

"Pizza," Angelo said. "On Spike. That was the eye of the hurricane, my friend. He's out in the storm again. I think he loves Jessica. He's got the pipe. Spike's given him a couple of lines and some weed. He's gone."

"Then get him out of there," I said. "Jessica's the bitch from hell. I did try to warn him but the poor sad fuck wouldn't listen. Did you bring any salt? No. Fair enough." I had to remember that Angelo was not an employee. He was just a useful kind of guy to have around. "He thought she really liked him. He thought it was going to happen with her." Then I remembered Electra. "Kind of. Actually, he's not too tightly wrapped on a good day."

As it turned out. My solid, sensible, solvent friend was none of these things in the end. I thought about feeling cheated or betrayed or something but the mood I was in, I had to admit it was my own fault. I'd never bothered to look, until I had to.

148

"Spike's taking the piss," Angelo said next. "He's a cruel man."

"Indeed," I said. "On speed. It's a winning combination every time. Why doesn't Miles just get up and leave?"

"I don't know," he said. "Where does he live?"

"Oh. Yeah. Well, here," I said. "For now." I'd forgotten about Sally and her bath buddy. And also about poor Electra's mother and the note when she got back from Harrogate. "Ask him to come and see me when you take the tray back. Say it's about the gig, so they don't think he's taking sides."

"The gig?"

"The gig … " I was forgetting Angelo had come in halfway through this. It seemed like he'd always been around. "We've got a band."

"Wow," he said. "That's cool."

"Yeah." I'd forgotten about the band. I'd forgotten about everything. If I survived this weekend I was going to do things differently. I was going to clean up. I was going to grow up, even. If I survived owing Spike Sharpe £800 I was going to get a job, a proper job with a salary and sick pay. I really was.

I cracked open a beer, to celebrate.

Angelo took the tray back. I carried on watching the Jessica story in the kitchen. I could see Spike stuffing more and more whiz up his nose. I could see Jessica sipping beer out of a glass. She was pretending to be a lady. It wouldn't last. Miles was propped up in a chair like a pile of crash test dummy parts. Some of the Sharpes were leaving. Angelo was talking to Miles. He was pointing down the garden. Miles didn't even look. He was busy doing another pipe.

I fell asleep. I didn't know at the time. I didn't think, I'm falling asleep, I should go and lie down. I just woke up when people started shouting. There was a big something happening. It was 2:14am. I thought about going up to the house, to see what was going on … or not. It seemed more sensible to wait. I would receive news soon enough.

And sure enough, here was Angelo, carrying something … Miles. He was carrying Miles in a fireman's lift.

"Oh shit," he was saying, over and over.

"What's up?" I said. I helped him lie Miles down on the bed in the summer house.

"It's Spike's wife," he said. "She came to find him. She just walked into the kitchen and started screaming at him. Miles is so pissed and your sister just punched Mrs. Spike. Maybe she took some speed or something … "

"Not necessarily," I said. "You don't know her like I do." But he wasn't listening.

" … and then Miles tried to punch Spike because he was yelling at her … "

"Was he? Good man."

" … and she was yelling back that she'd had enough and the children never saw him … "

O.K. Spike was yelling at his wife. Shame.

" … and it all got totally mad, man, because some

of the brothers came back because they thought Mrs Spike was going to cause a pile of trouble and now they're all yelling and fighting. And Miles got punched and he went down like a dead man."

"I shouldn't worry too much," I said. "It's probably just another phase he's going through."

"We should take him to the hospital," Angelo said. He really was a sweetheart.

"He'll be alright. We can't get out without going through the house. It's not safe." I could see the fight through the French windows. "Let's wait and see what happens next. You'd better bunk up with Miles. He won't mind. How about a bedtime beer?"

I'd woken up on Saturday morning with a house, a girlfriend, a band and a future.

I would be waking up on Monday with none of these things.

But at least I had a sleeping bag. Experience had taught me to keep the summer house well stocked. I found some paracetamol, knocked back a handful and settled down on the verandah for a kip. We'd see about tomorrow in the morning.

15

The morning: dew on my sleeping bag, clear skies, soft sunshine, Angelo on the verandah steps whistling a little Bolivian folk tune … and Miles. Miles lurching out of the summer house, insisting he had to go to work.

I told him it would be the end of his teaching career if he did. I'd never seen him looking worse. I'd never seen anyone looking worse. He thought a quick wash and some clean clothes would turn it around.

"It won't," I said. I pointed out that any clean clothes we might have between us were in the house. The house was out of the question. The blowsy flowery cheesecloth shirt and pink flares were definitely weekend wear only. I offered to call in sick for him. "Even if you'd just put that on you couldn't go to work in it," I said. "And it's not just the clothes. Have you looked in a mirror recently?"

"He's right," Angelo said. "You don't want to scare the little children."

Miles started slamming round the garden, shouting something about having to carry on. We ignored him.

"So what are you going to do?" Angelo asked me.

"Right now? I'm going to sit here until I think of a plan."

Which might take some time. Meanwhile, there were a lot of things I could do. I could go down to Louis' to pick up the gear but I didn't have a van. Or anywhere to put it. Or, in fact, the keys to Sally's van, even if I could remember where I'd put that. Or them. I could go down to the Job Centre but I needed a wash and a change of clothes before I presented myself anywhere. And also maybe two or three days to straighten out first.

Miles was now banging on the French doors, shouting that he had to get in, he had to carry on …

"Maybe they went out," Angelo said.

Maybe. We'd find out soon enough. I could go down to Louis' and pick up the money for the gig. Then I could go to Scope and get a change of clothes. This was sounding better. Then I could check if Jessica really was out, or dead or something and get my stuff out of the house and set up here. Miles had given up on the French doors and was heading our way. He was still shouting that he had to carry on, that he was a prisoner in a back garden, that his dad had just died and had we no sympathy …

"How can I carry on if I'm trapped … trapped," he yelled.

I was bored with Miles. I think he was bored with himself. I thought he was keeping this up because he was actually enjoying exercising his unwrapped self, letting rip for the first time ever. But I was bored with it now. I was even bored with the awful irony of Dr Johnson's health directive for his youngest son. That'll teach you to meddle, I thought, as the deconstructed Miles, standing by a tea rose, lit his first pipe of the day. Angelo sighed.

"What are we going to do with him?" he said.

"I think he should go to work," I said. "It's what he wants. Hey, Miles? The only way out is over the back wall. I'll give you a leg if you like."

Mike was bringing bottles up from the cellar in a wire shopping basket. He looked like an alkie on a trip to the supermarket.

"I've put your gear downstairs," he said. "Has the law caught up with you yet?"

"No. What's the charge?"

"Taking away a van without the owner's permission. I've had Miles' bird on the blower. It's a bit of a mess, mate, isn't it?"

"Maybe. You didn't pay us for the gig." I saw him drawing breath, about to start listing the damage from the fight, the loss of earnings on a Saturday night, the storage of the gear, the hire of his drum kit ... "The fight was fuck all to do with us," I said. "Come on, Mike. Look at me. Would I be here if I wasn't in the shit?"

He was a decent bloke. He paid me half. It was enough for now.

I took Angelo into Scope and treated him to a new shirt. I picked up a pinstripe suit and a Calvin Klein T-shirt: £17. Thanks very much.

We went back to the house. I rang the bell. Then I banged on the front door: 10:53 and still no answer. I got one of the many spare keys I keep hidden around out from under a loose tile in the porch and opened the front door. Still no-one.

"I don't like this," Angelo said. "I think something bad has happened here."

"Something bad always happens when Jessica comes out of rehab," I said. "It's a pattern. Let's get what we need and get out before she turns up."

But I didn't think she would. The house had that gone away feel about it. We were sorting out some plates and extra blankets, beers, underwear, the goldfish when the doorbell rang. It was Luke, bringing Miles back.

"He was trying to hitch a lift in Church Street," he said.

Church Street, Stoke Newington? I couldn't be arsed to enquire.

"I tried," Miles said. "God knows I tried, God only knows how I … " etc.

"What's up with him?" Luke said.

"It's alright," I said. "He's turned into a B movie, that's all. Have another pipe, Miles. Work your way through it. Can you give us a hand with this lot, Luke?"

Which was how come we were all sitting on the verandah steps … me, Miles, Luke, Angelo … by Monday lunchtime.

But where was Jessica?

Not that it mattered. I had to move out anyway.

"Where do you live, Luke?" I said.

"With my gran in her flat in Hackney. I split up from my girlfriend."

What do you call a musician without a girlfriend? Homeless. It's not a joke. It's true.

"What about you, Angelo?" I said.

"I was thinking about going back to Bolivia," he said. "It hasn't worked out for me here."

"So we're all homeless," I said. "Technically."

Shame about the tour. The timing was perfect. Still, there were things that needed sorting here and now. There was Dr Johnson's funeral. There was Miles' sick note. And there was £800 to raise by Friday.

"Beer, anyone?" I said.

Technically homeless was turning out well, better than any other kind of homeless I'd ever seen. Or been. We … me, Luke, Angelo … sat in the sunshine, smoking, drinking beer, admiring the garden. The only disturbance was Miles fumbling with his pipe.

"I might go into horticulture," I said. "I've always liked plants."

"I have," I said, after an incredulous silence. "I planted most of this."

"Really?" Luke said. "I never knew that."

"I never knew you lived with your grandmother in Hackney." It was the first thing Miles had said since his God knows I tried speech … and it was sensible. Cannabis in a crisis, then. I wondered how much he had left. It seemed to be working … for now, anyway. "I thought you lived in Lewisham."

"From now on we're going to tell each other stuff," I said. "For example, both you two," meaning Miles and Luke, "come from big families."

"I didn't know that," Luke said. "I mean, I know I do. Obviously."

"So you've got more in common than you think," I carried on. I was getting into it now. We were talking, really talking about things that mattered. "What about you, Angelo?"

"I come from a big family," he said. "I have four brothers and three sisters. But I think the horticulture market is a bit stale right now. Too many TV shows."

"People always need a gardener," I said.

"My gran doesn't," Luke said. "She's got a balcony."

"Alright, then. One person here has a grandmother who doesn't need a gardener. But apart from that ..."

"People always need their hair cutting," Miles said. Sensible comment No.2. Very good.

"It would take too long to train," I said. "I need £800 by Friday or I'll be going for a long walk in the Thames."

"We can help you," Angelo said. The others nodded.

"Great," I said. "Do any of you have £800 you can lend me?" Of course they didn't. "Or any ideas?"

"He might be joking," Miles said, which was only

slightly stupid. If you were him. It was cosmically stupid if you were anyone else.

"He's not," Luke said. "I know he's my brother but he's the meanest, maddest bastard this side of Blackheath."

"So who lives the other side of Blackheath?" I said. My God, I was never going there again.

"He never lets anything go," Luke went on. "He says it's the only way to run a business. I've seen him hammer a bloke's fingers, and that was on the way home from school."

"But he doesn't need the money," Miles said, still in touch.

"That's got fuck all to do with it," I said. "What I want to know is, why didn't you ever mention anything about your family, Luke?" That way we might've been more careful. Or sacked you. Or accepted a tour of Botswana and left a day early …

"Well, would you?" he said. "The last band I was in … "

"Please," I said. "Stop there. I have to face up to it. I'm going to have to leave the country."

"You could go to see your mother in Ireland," Miles said.

"Of course. Because Spike will have absolutely no idea where she lives, will he?"

Miles was smiling. Suddenly it worried me.

"Can I come too?" he said.

"I never knew your mother lived in Ireland," Luke said. "Are you Irish, then?"

"I could ask my uncle if you could play at his

hotel," Angelo said. "A summer season."

A summer season in Bolivia?

"Do they have bands in Bolivia?" I said. "I thought it was all ponchos and pan pipes."

"I'm not from Bolivia," he said. "I was making it up. I'm from Van, in Turkey."

"Why did you say you were from Bolivia?" Luke said.

"You know ... " Angelo shrugged.

"Er ... no?" I said.

"The illegal immigrant thing, the war, the P.K.K, bombers ... it's easier to be someone else."

This was a strange revelation ... but then maybe not so strange. He was right. It was easier to be someone else.

"A summer season in Van," I said. "When can we leave?"

We decided to visit Luke's Gran in Hackney. He said she'd cook us something to eat. We went by bus, on the top deck. I rang Miles' doctor and made an appointment for him. I rang the school and told them about his father. I rang Heidi, to ask about the funeral. It was on Thursday.

"He's taking it hard," I said. "He'll call you when he's strong enough."

Luke's grandmother cooked us a roast chicken. We sat on her balcony and watched the neighbourhood kids beating the crap out of each other in the car park. I offered to do her some tubs. I was really taking the horticulture idea seriously. Luke told her

I was in the shit with Spike.

"They're a bad lot, those Sharpes," she said. "There's madness on that side of the family, proper madness. Raving, some of them. Have you told your friend about Uncle Thomas, Lukey?" And without waiting for confirmation and refusing to be shushed she carried on with the grisly story of Thomas the Tool, Luke's father's brother. It ended with him in Broadmoor. "I'm the other side," she said. "The Murphys. We've got a few stories as well."

I said I thought we should be leaving.

We … me, Miles, Angelo … headed back to Clapham. We could see the police knocking on the front door of the house from the top of the street. We went round the back. I was just about to break out some beers when there was a scrabbling noise and a copper stuck his head over the wall.

"Excuse me," he said. "I'm looking for a Mr Sharpe. A Mr Spike Sharpe?"

We shook our heads.

"Last seen at this address?" the copper said.

We shrugged.

"Turkish," Angelo said. We shrugged again.

He left.

This was good.

I sat on the verandah steps with Angelo while Miles lay face down in the grass, wondering what it could mean … but whatever it did mean, it had to be better than whatever it was that was happening before. So it was definitely an improvement.

We talked about the possibility of leaving for Van before Friday. I'd be safe there, Angelo said. We talked about the kebab shop he'd been working in, the room he'd been living in upstairs.

"Five of us, three beds," he said. "It's another world, man."

I asked him if his name really was Angelo. He said it was. His father had wanted something different for him. There was such a stab of pathos in this I wanted to weep. I looked at Miles, who appeared to be grazing. I wondered if his father had wanted something different for him, and how this could be reflected in his choice of name: Miles away? Miles from nowhere? Twenty-four Miles from Tulsa? Except that was hours. Anyway, it all seemed a bit distant.

"How do we get there?" I asked Angelo.

"We fly to Antalya and take a bus. It's the cheapest way."

"What about a piano? And drums for Luke?"

"You tell my uncle what you want. He can get you anything, believe me."

"So is it a big tourist place?"

"No."

"So why would your uncle want a band?"

"It's hard to explain. You'll see when you get there."

"What if Spike came looking for me?"

"He won't. No-one goes to Van unless there is no other way."

161

We carried on sitting on the verandah steps. It was getting dark. The house was dark. So the house was empty. And there were three people living in a shed at the end of the garden. What a joke ... and all because some fucked-up guilty dead man wanted to make up ground from beyond the grave. Suddenly I hated him. Suddenly I wanted to beat the crap out of his sad and sorry son, just for being so fucking ...

"How come you were at the party?" I asked Angelo.

I had to think about something else because I really could stamp on him. I really could mash his stupid face into the grass, break his fucking freckled neck ...

"I walk a lot at night," he said. "I hate that stinking room."

So my best offer was coming from someone who happened to be passing, who'd walked in off the street two days ago. I liked Angelo.

"We're not going to make it to Van, are we?" I said. I lit a cigarette. I only had two left. Maybe I should think about making a change, giving up. I rattled the two lonely little fags in their empty pack. They'd be useless nails for anyone's coffin. They were much too bendy ... but as it turned out, they were the pins that were holding Miles' life together. I looked at him, still face down in the dark. And there was Dr Johnson, face up in a refrigerator. I wondered if the light stayed on when they closed the door. "I've really fucked up, haven't I?" I said.

I could tell Angelo didn't know what to say next.

I sighed, to let him know I knew. It was all so utterly pointless.

16

Tuesday morning and Jessica still wasn't back. I went in to check the mail, check the answer machine. I put some washing on while I was there. I was too broke to go to the launderette and we had to turn out well for the funeral. I figured she wouldn't mind that much.

Angelo had taken charge of Miles. They were sitting together in a corner of the garden, talking quietly about life, death, the meaning of blah blah blah bollocks. I preferred the company of my laundry basket but I was grateful to Angelo. I couldn't have done it myself. I just wanted to punch the stupid whining little fucker.

Tuesday evening: all the laundry was done. I set up the ironing board outside the French windows and ran an extension lead out from the nearest socket. I was outside the house, technically, so the worst she could do was unplug the iron. If she came back. I worked quickly, just in case. Then I went to fetch some chips. Miles was refusing to move from his corner of the garden. He said it was the only place he felt safe. I personally thought he'd smoked so much neat weed he'd lost the use of his legs. Still, what did I care? At least he was on grass. If he died I could dig a hole next to him and roll him in.

Wednesday morning and still no Jessica. Miles was now resident in his corner. Angelo had laid out a rug and put a bottle of water there, a cup, a box of tissues, a packet of custard creams, some back copies of Cosmopolitan. I cooked breakfast in the kitchen but we ate it on the verandah. I left the French windows open. That way we could hear the phone if Jessica tried to call the land line. I thought about going down to the Job Centre but decided to leave it till after the funeral.

Wednesday pm: caught Miles taking a dump under the jasmine. He said he couldn't leave his corner, not even to crap. I nearly strangled him. Angelo managed to pull me off before he was completely dead. He's got marks on his neck. I'm going to have to find him a cravat for tomorrow. And he's scorching the night-scented stocks with his vile piss.

Wednesday evening: Miles still in his corner, insensible with weed. I sat on the verandah with Angelo and discussed my date with the Thames on Friday … but still no Jessica, which kind of means no Spike either. Maybe. Angelo asked me what I was going to do. I don't know. What can I do? I haven't got enough money to get past Croydon. And then what do I do? I think I'd prefer death to life in a bus shelter. So the next time I'm watching a documentary about the Nazis or Sarajevo or whatever, ie people not running away in time, I'll know why they don't. It's not that easy.

We're using the house again, with the summer house as a bedroom for two. There's no reason not to. There never was, which was why Jessica ended up paying me to caretake the place while she was indisposed. Which was most of the time. It was a good arrangement.

I rang Heidi, to ask her if the Johnson family would like their son and brother back. She said they were all far too busy with the funeral to cope with messy Miles. I said maybe after the funeral? She said they'd all be far too busy dealing with the will, the sale of the family house, sorting out the linen and anyway she had to go. Good-bye.

I went shopping and Angelo cooked dinner. He's good at couscous. We ate in the kitchen. It was good to be back, in a way. I raided Jessica's best wine and found some Cristal. I knew I wouldn't be replacing it … but then if she wasn't here she wouldn't know. I went back and got another bottle. We needed a proper send-off for Dr Johnson. Or me. I went back and got another bottle. Angelo took some down to Miles. He didn't want it. He said he'd found the answer. I think we need to discover cannabis before we're seventeen. That way we don't make such screaming prats of ourselves.

Thursday morning, and we're trying to get Miles ready. He is filthy and fighting us off. I'd planned on taking him to pick up his sick note on the way to the crematorium. I thought his G.P. might prescribe some tranquillisers, or at least a shot of something to get him through the service. Angelo thinks we should avoid all contact with the medical profession. He thinks they'll section him on sight. Why hadn't I thought of this? It could be the solution … but even I couldn't do that to him.

But … ha. I have an idea. Doctors are like junkies: they hang out together. I tell Miles that if he doesn't get a grip he's going to get spotted by his father's friends. They might wrestle him to the ground and put him in a straitjacket, out of a sense of duty to dear old Dr Johnson. It would be no more than he deserved. It works. He says he wants coffee, coffee and a shower and a shave. I knew he wasn't that lost, the shit. Angelo goes with him, to help him shave. His hands are shaking.

The next thing is the copper drops by again, to see if Spike's around. I'm looking a lot better than I was the last time and luckily he doesn't recognise me. I tell him I have no idea where Spike is. He says he hopes the Turks living at the end of the garden have all the proper work permits. It's a threat, to see if I cave in and cough up. I say that two of them have left already and the third is going soon. And I still don't know where Spike is. He says he'll be back.

And then, just as I'm shutting the door, Luke turns up. He actually passes the policeman at the gate: a major Sharpe and the cop walks right by him. It's a wonder they ever catch anyone. But never mind about that. He's brought the best possible news. Spike's wife has shopped him, a revenge thing, for being such a useless bastard. And also violent, as it turns out. I don't know why Luke is so shocked by this. I always thought wives got the worst of it. So Spike has done a runner with Jessica and Mrs Spike is busy telling the whole story of his life of crime to anyone who'll listen, mainly The Daily Mail and Scotland Yard: fraud, extortion, robbery, drugs and even some death.

"Did you know he was that … " I search for the word.

"Instigated?" Luke suggests. "That's what they say, isn't it?"

No, but never mind. "Did you?" I say.

He makes a face, a face that tells me he did.

"That's the business," he says.

"So what happens about the £800 now?"

"You'll be alright. Spike's the only killer in the family."

The crematorium was looking as good as it could and it still looked like a bad place to end up: begonias in a war grave arrangement, a tight little Celtic knot of slimy concrete pavement where veiled widows blind with weeping could exercise their grief, colliding like disconnected bumper cars … but I was getting hysterical. There was a dangerously high level of doom about the place. It was getting to me.

I looked around for something cheerful.

On one side a screen of silver birch was failing to screen off the dog food factory next door. And opposite, the upstairs windows of a '70s housing estate stared rudely over a chain link fence. A police car went howling by, and then an ambulance. There was nothing. It was totally dismal.

The Chapel of Rest and Incineration was

something like a hacienda. Even the chimney up which Dr Johnson would shortly be disappearing had a Mexican look, like we were in L.A. suddenly. Maybe it made it easier to see death as just another country. Or maybe the council thought a Western theme would somehow soften the impact, like dead actors get up after a shoot out and go for a spot of lunch. Whatever, it was not good and we … me, Miles, Angelo, Luke … all lost our nerve. I felt it collectively go.

Luke was holding on to Miles. I pulled Angelo back.

"This is a mistake," I said. "There's going to be trouble before the end. How d'you think Miles looks?" Angelo raised an eyebrow. We'd done our best to tidy him up but the fight was only four days back. "Yeah. So how do I look?" Angelo didn't answer. "That bad?" He nodded. And Luke had taken three clear batterings, as opposed to my odd punch here and there. I realised we should've stopped to buy darkest black wraps on the way to the crem. Too late. Still, I couldn't be expected to think of everything.

"We'd better go in," I said.

Something else I hadn't thought of: that the chapel of rest would be empty. Or almost empty, but there were so few people it was more empty than if there'd been no-one. I'd been thinking we could hide out at the back … behind a row of big old boys from medical school perhaps, too busy holding back the tears to notice the disintegrated Miles and his loyal chums … and then slip away discreetly for a private pint. Or something. Fat chance. There was a line of Johnsons at the front and a scattering of whoever and that was it. Everyone turned around to look when we walked in. We were totally visible.

The brother who wasn't Michael pushed out of his pew, treading on his family. His face was turning that give-away shade of pure pillar box red. He was going to start another fight. He kind of ran towards us, waving his hands. He had to stop us getting any further. He had to stop Miles.

"What are you doing here?" he said. To me.

"I've brought Miles to his father's funeral," I said. What did he think I was doing?

"You're not invited," he said. "Or these other people."

"D'you mean Miles?" I said.

"We don't want a fuss," he said, which didn't answer my question. Everyone was still staring. A door opened down by the coffin and a man came out. I saw him check his watch. He wanted to start the service.

"We'll just sit down at the back," I said. "You won't know we're there."

"But we don't want you here," he said. "This is a family affair."

Which made me think of the song. I love that song. And then I thought, why am I even trying to talk to this arsehole? I could hear Sly singing away in my head, which somehow made Miles' brother seem even more of an arsehole, the worst kind of arsehole … a black hole of an arsehole, even. I was just about to point this out to him when Miles said:

"Where is everyone?"

Michael was coming towards us now. He was looking worried.

"Just let them sit down," he said to his pillar box brother. "We have to start."

"But where is everyone?" Miles said.

"Mum wanted to get it over with," not Michael said. "It was her decision to push on with it. We don't want a fuss."

"You don't want a fuss?" Miles said. "What exactly the fuck do you mean by that?"

"Matthew, just let them sit down," Michael said.

But Matthew was beyond backing down. He'd been expecting trouble and he was bloody well going to have it. Or a heart attack. I hated him. So no change there, then.

"How about we leave Miles with you and wait outside?" Angelo said.

"Who the hell are you to organise my father's funeral?" Matthew said. Actually, he was shouting by now and doing that red to purple thing again.

"But where is everyone?" Miles said. Again. The man at the front coughed, to let us know we were taking up funeral time. "Why isn't Janice here? Or Uncle Charlie?"

"We're sending out cards," Michael said. He was looking wretched now.

"You're sending out fucking cards?" Miles yelled.

"Fucking cards?" This was louder. "Fucking cards?" And this was the loudest noise I'd ever heard him make, including through a trombone. Matthew stepped towards him. He really, really wanted to beat the crap out of him. I could just tell. And Luke, our fight expert, thought so too because he stepped in front of Miles to protect him. God only knows what years of grinding family life had done to them … look at me and Jessica as one small example. Whoever would get that?

"It was what Mum wanted," Michael said. It was obvious he thought it was total crap too but he'd gone along with it anyway.

"What about what Dad wanted?" Miles bellowed. "What about what his friends want? What about what I want?"

"Oh, of course," Matthew said, spitting sarcasm. "How stupid of us. It's always got to be about what you want, hasn't it?" But he didn't step in any closer. I think he knew Luke was a professional.

"No it fucking hasn't," Miles said. "That's just your way of justifying what a miserable fucking git you've always been."

I felt we were sliding into an old argument. The man at the front was talking to Heidi and the sisters, saying they were running out of time, another party would be arriving soon, they'd slotted in the Johnsons as a special favour …

"Look," I said. "Why don't you do the funeral and have the fight after? They've got to get on."

But Miles had heard the slotted in conversation.

172

"Oh my God," he wailed. "Poor Dad, poor Dad, oh God oh God he's been slotted … " etc.

It's a strange word when you think about it, which of course we all did because now he was shouting it over and over again … slotted, slotted, slotted … until it made no sense. Angelo looked to me for clarification. Slotted? What was this slotted?

"How could you?" Miles was yelling at Matthew. "How could you let her slot him? Dad was right. She's a fucking old bitch."

Matthew, Michael and the sisters were appalled by this, horrified, like it had never occurred to them. I didn't believe it. Heidi was still sitting in her pew, eyes front, but the sisters were on their way over.

"Why don't you just go away and leave us alone?" one of them said to Miles.

"Yes," the other one said. "Where were you all week anyway? You can't just turn up and expect to change everything."

"She's a fucking useless old bitch," Miles said. This was getting us nowhere. The man at the front was exiting through his official's door. He'd had enough.

"It was Dad who made her useless," Matthew said. "If he hadn't kept her on the Valium for all those years … "

Now Miles was appalled, horrified. So were Michael and the sisters. It had clearly never occurred to them that their mother was a prescription junky. Oh dear. There was no way there was going to be time to finish the family argument and turn Dr Johnson urn-size now. This was a whole new chapter.

"It's true," Matthew said. "It bloody is true. It bloody well is."

He wanted someone to argue with him, to say no it wasn't true so he could hurt them somehow but everyone just looked at him, waiting to see what he'd do next. Shut the fuck up? Drop dead? Sadly not. Now he had our attention he was going to empty out the whole bag of shite, all over the chapel floor.

"You had no idea, did you?" he said. "Years and years of Valium addiction and you wonder why she found it hard to cope. He kept writing the prescriptions, to keep it quiet. And I had to cover for her because she couldn't own up to her little habit. You don't know what I've been through. You've no idea what it's like being the eldest son, no idea what it's like to have to carry the burden of responsibility, all the lies and deceit while you … "

"My fucking brother used to give me that crap," Luke said.

" … carried on as though we were one big happy family while I … "

"One big what?" one of the sisters said.

" … was tied to her trolley in every supermarket in Surrey in case she tried her shoplifting trick again."

"What … happy … family?" the other sister suddenly screamed at him, right in his face, which did at least stall him for a couple of beats.

And then the door down by the coffin opened again. The official stepped out. He had someone with him, a woman. She had more authority, you could tell. And shoulder pads, possibly the only woman in the northern hemisphere still left with shoulder pads. She moved over to Dr Johnson and rested her hand on his lid.

"Good morning," she said. "I'm Dulcie Veneer. We really must start the service now."

I suppose she'd seen it all before. And she was right, of course, but the Johnsons weren't listening. Now they were yelling and crying and shoving each other while Heidi sat in her pew, eyes front, pretending none of it was happening. Actually, maybe she wasn't pretending. Maybe for her it really wasn't happening. Maybe in Heidi's world of Valium nothing ever really happened.

"Excuse me," Dulcie said. "If we don't start now I shall have no choice but to ask you to remove your loved one until a future date for cremation can be arranged."

"Yes," her colleague said. "There are other people waiting."

The Johnsons still weren't listening. They were locked into their family misery, currently somewhere back in the 1980s, trawling through an amazing array of old scores unsettled. Now they'd started they couldn't stop. Their misery was all that mattered.

"So if you could notify your funeral director," Dulcie was saying. "Unless you would prefer to simply skip the ceremony and proceed with the cremation?"

She moved over to a kind of serving hatch set in

the wall and opened the dinky little doors. It was the control panel for the conveyor belt.

I saw Heidi raise a scraggy claw. She was nodding yes, push the button.

Dulcie looked around the chapel, hoping, maybe, for a second opinion. She caught my eye. I shrugged. Don't ask me. Heidi was still nodding yes, do it, her horrible hand jabbing at the air: do it, do it, just get rid of the old bastard.

It was a brave decision. Dulcie pushed the button.

The velvet curtains covering the entrance to the furnace jerked open and Dr Johnson started to roll. Somehow music started too. There was so much noise from the fighting family members I couldn't catch the tune … The Wind Beneath My Wings? Surely not.

But no-one was listening anyway. They hadn't even noticed their father was finally departing. And he'd nearly made it. He was halfway through the hole in the wall … and you'll never know that you're my hero … when Miles realised what was happening.

Luke and Angelo saw something was wrong … even more wrong than everything that was already horribly wrong … and tried to grab him as he tried to push through his brothers and sisters and do … whatever. Stop the coffin? Give a speech? Read something from The Prophet? But they were too slow and there were too many Johnsons in the way and Miles had that strength of a madman thing going again. Somehow he managed to get past all of them … at one point I swear he levitated over a pew, kind of Kill Bill style … but it was too late. By the time he made it to the front of the chapel Dr Johnson had gone.

It wouldn't have made any difference. What was he going to do with his dead father anyway? Take him out for a last drink? But Miles clearly hadn't thought this one through because he hurled himself onto the conveyor belt shouting Dad Dad Dad no no no. Luke and Angelo tried to grab his ankles but he was kicking like the worst bitch of a mare. Dulcie was frantically pushing the button, over and over again, in an attempt to prevent an embarrassing mix-up but it seemed there was no way to stop the thing once it had started. I could tell this was a career first for her.

Miles was almost through the hole in the wall before Luke managed to get a hold on his ankles and pull him back out. He was yelling and thrashing around and Matthew and Michael were punching each other and one of the sisters was screaming law suits at poor old Dulcie and the other one was shaking Heidi and yelling something about the Girl Guides … God Almighty, I'd had enough of them.

And all the while The Wind Beneath My Wings was playing through the crap P.A. I hoped Dr Johnson had a well-developed sense of humour.

Time for a cig.

17

I sat on a bench by a sad little squad of begonias and closed my eyes.

What a total fucking nightmare.

But it was over now, more or less, and soon we'd all be in a pub somewhere and quite soon after that, God willing, everything would start to blur nicely and ...

I opened my eyes. I was being approached by a drunk in a school blazer. It was buttoned up wrong.

"Are you finished in there now?" he said. He was Irish. I'd known it before he even opened his mouth. "You've run over, haven't you? I'm here for Billy." He pointed to a piebald hearse ... primer grey, matt black ... pulled up in the car park.

"Right," I said. "Billy."

"Did you know him?" he said. "I thought you was with the last lot. They're taking an awful long time about it. I've got all me songs to do, and readings ... for Billy. He asked me."

"I think they're done," I said.

"That's good. Because it would be an awful shame not to do it proper. For Billy."

Luke and Angelo were coming over. They had Miles pinned between them. He was quiet now but they were hanging on to him all the same, just in case.

"Not many for their fella either," Billy's mate said.

"No," I said. "Probably don't mention that, alright?"

Luke and Angelo sat Miles down on the bench. They sat either side of him, still hanging on.

"She is a fucking old bitch," Miles said.

"That's no way to talk of the dead," Billy's mate said. "Drink, anyone?" He had a half bottle of brandy, half empty. "I thought I'd treat myself," he said. "It's a special day."

He took a mouthful and offered it around.

"No thanks," I said.

"She's not fucking dead," Miles said. "That's the problem."

The rest of the Johnsons were leaving the crem, shuffling along like zombies ... so that would be twice dead for Heidi, or even thrice. It was hard to say ... like people on the news at the airport coming back from a surprise holiday earthquake. Billy's mate was blind drunk already and he could see it.

"Someone died sudden?" he said.

"Not really." I lit a cigarette. The Johnsons got into their cars, one each, and drove away. They didn't wave good-bye. Billy's hearse pulled up to the coffin-in door round the side of the hacienda. There wasn't a coffin-out door, of course. It was one way traffic only. Dr Johnson was probably the closest anyone ever came to making the return

179

journey. "It's your go," I said.

Miles was looking over at Billy in his box. It looked like he'd made it himself. The undertaker and his assistant were trying to fit it through the door.

"I told him," Billy's mate said. "It's too big. Now look. It won't go in."

Luke turned his head away. He wanted to laugh. Angelo was chewing on his bottom lip. The undertaker's assistant had scraped his hand against the door frame. He was trying to hold Billy up with one hand while he sucked on his bleeding knuckles. It was never going to work. The undertaker was swearing at him … hold the bloody thing up. I'm going to bloody drop it …

"Why've they only got two people?" Miles said. "They need more than that."

"They're not professionals," Billy's mate said. "It's a favour. You have to keep the cost down somehow."

The amateur assistant couldn't hang on any longer. He let go of his end and Billy crashed to the ground.

"It's the melamine, you see," Billy's mate said. "Weighs a hell of a lot more than pine. He was very green minded, Billy. It's old kitchen worktops from the tip."

Miles was never going to see the funny side of this. He thought we shouldn't be laughing … at Billy's coffin, at the undertaker's assistant, at Billy's mate tarted up in his primary school blazer with his hair stuck down for best … at any of it. I could kind of see why. We made a thing of lighting cigarettes, to distract ourselves from Billy's mate's vocal warm-up … Shalamar, me darling, Shalamar etc. But not Miles, of course. He was still captive between Luke and Angelo, biting on the end of his thumb.

"We should get you some patches," I said.

"Here's that woman," Luke said.

Dulcie Veneer was marching towards us. She slipped and almost fell on the slimy Celtic knot … woopsie … but then she didn't. We were already giggling like a bunch of girls. This made it much, much worse.

"We're ready for you now," she said to Billy's mate. The melamine coffin was still outside the crem. It had come apart. I was glad he'd missed seeing Billy being lifted from the wreckage … but I was more glad I'd missed it.

"So what's he in now?" Billy's mate said. "A roll of old carpet?"

I wondered if this had been one of Billy's ideas, before melamine, after bubble wrap.

"We've provided a very nice cardboard coffin," Dulcie said. "At no extra charge."

"But is it recycled?" he said.

"We really must start now," she said, "unless you would prefer to simply proceed with the cremation?"

Poor Dulcie. She was having a bad day. Another hearse was already pulling into the car park, and then a line of limos: a stiff with money to burn.

Better not keep them waiting. I could see she was about to lose it.

"And if you wouldn't mind," she said to me, and pointed to a sign stuck in the back of the begonias: Thank you for not Smoking. Which was all about trying to save something of her dignity and nothing to do with our fags.

At this very moment the chimney up above the pink stucco crematorium exhaled … whoomph … and a great big puff of Dr Johnson smoke drifted off into the stinking diesel soup that is commonly mistaken for air in London. Should we wave? We weren't sure. But it looked like the biggest, meanest, most toxic cigarette you ever saw. Miles thought so too.

"Thank you for not smoking?" he said … little pause for the total lunacy of this to really sink in … "Thank you for not fucking smoking?" Another pause while he watched his father drift. "Are you fucking joking? What the fuck's that then?"

He couldn't point at the chimney because Luke and Angelo were still hanging on to him. We were all looking anyway, possibly slightly shocked and appalled, even Dulcie who was in such a hurry. It was really bad timing.

And then, just to really screw things up, there was some kind of weird downdraft and Dr Johnson started to sink. And then more smoke came out of the chimney and didn't even bother going up at all before it kind of flopped down on the crem and it became totally obvious that the reason the pink stucco was so filthy was because this happened a lot. The hacienda was black with the soot of the deceased.

"That chimney's not drawing right," Billy's mate said to Dulcie. "When did you last get it swept?"

"That's it," Miles said. "I've had enough. For fuck's sake, give me a fag someone."

And that was it: it was over, thank Christ. We made Miles promise on his life to never give up the fags again, not while he was within a hundred mile radius of any of us, anyway.

We sat in Louis' and totalled up the damage: one domicile, two girlfriends, half a band and an entire family. Jessica didn't count. No-one minded losing her.

Mike came up from the cellar.

"Someone's been trying to get hold of you," he said.

"Like?"

"That agent bloke. He came to the gig. Guinness?"

It seemed like a good choice.

"What d'you think he wants?" Luke said. He was thinking personal injury claims, loss of earnings, psychological damage, that kind of stuff. Miles went off to the lav. Should we follow him?

"He just needs a piss," I said. I put my mobile on the bar. "Did anyone actually see Mr Bonwit getting punched?"

"You'd better check it out," Angelo said.

He was right. I picked it up … two messages. Only two? I was losing my touch. The first one was from Jessica. She was at an undisclosed foreign location. Could I look after the house till whenever? I suppose so. Why not? It was always a good arrangement. The second was from Mr Bonwit. Could I ring him as soon as I got this message? He sounded alright. Still …

"He wants me to call him," I said. Miles came back from the lav.

"Then call him," he said. "You've run out of loo roll, Mike."

Loo roll? How quaint. But Miles did seem genuinely like his old self again. We should celebrate.

"Mike? Four more, please," I said. "And then I'll call him."

Mr Bonwit wanted to see us. I told him we'd come to his office at four. He wanted to sign us up to his agency. He'd come to our gig expecting to see the same old pointless polished jazz standards. What he'd got was raw, inventive, unique. He loved us. How did we manage to play two songs at the same time? It was so new, so entertaining, so would we like a summer residency?

Yes, yes, yes.

"In Beirut?" He thought I'd hang up on him.

"Beirut?" I said. It was a dream come true … "Why not? But how are the Lebanese on the Kurdish question? We've got a percussionist now."

"They're fine," he said. "Very friendly, tolerant people. Your percussionist will be fine. No more money, of course, but fine. And maybe I can swing a slot at the Elat jazz festival for you. You like Elat?"

"Mr Bonwit, I love it. All that … sand."

I went back into Louis'.

"Put your pints down, boys," I said. "You're not going to believe this."